Bac...

A colle... ...tles
from one of the world's best-loved
romance authors. Harlequin is proud to
bring back these sought after titles and
present them as one cherished collection.

BETTY NEELS: COLLECTOR'S EDITION

HARLEQUIN®

Betty Neels spent her childhood and youth in Devonshire before training as a nurse and midwife. She was an army nursing sister during the war, married a Dutchman, and subsequently lived in Holland for fourteen years. She now lives with her husband in Dorset, and has a daughter and grandson. Her hobbies are reading, animals, old buildings and, of course, writing. Betty started to write on retirement from nursing, incited by a lady in a library bemoaning the lack of romantic novels.

Mrs. Neels is always delighted to receive fan letters, but would truly appreciate it if they could be directed to Harlequin Mills & Boon Ltd., 18-24 Paradise Road, Richmond, Surrey, TW9 1SR, England.

Books by Betty Neels

BETTY NEELS

CASSANDRA BY CHANCE

COLLECTOR'S EDITION

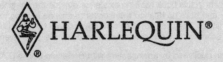

HARLEQUIN®

TORONTO • NEW YORK • LONDON
AMSTERDAM • PARIS • SYDNEY • HAMBURG
STOCKHOLM • ATHENS • TOKYO • MILAN • MADRID
PRAGUE • WARSAW • BUDAPEST • AUCKLAND

ISBN 0-373-83390-3

CASSANDRA BY CHANCE

First North American Publication 1973.

CHAPTER ONE

THE steamer from Oban drew into the island's small jetty, deserted and unwelcoming, shrouded as it was in the chilly October rain and buffeted by an even chillier wind from the north. The few passengers it had brought over from the mainland disembarked smartly, bidding each other good-day as they went in cheerful voices which paid no heed to the weather. But the last passenger left the boat slowly, as though reluctant to exchange its shelter for the rain-swept quay. She was a young woman, obviously a stranger, sensibly dressed in a thick tweed coat and high leather boots. She carried a hold-all over one arm and clutched the head scarf tied over her rain-drenched hair with a gloved hand. One of the passengers had carried her case for her; he put it down now beside her with a smile and she smiled her thanks in return, a smile which transformed her ordinary face, so that the man looked at her a second time with rather more interest than he had shown.

'Being met?' he asked.

She nodded, 'Yes, thank you,' and she didn't add anything, so that after a moment or so he said: 'Well, so long,' and walked away towards the huddle of houses around the end of the quay. Cassandra Darling watched him go and then turned her attention to her surroundings. She was quite a tall girl with a face which her mother had once hopefully described as *jolie-laide*, for her hazel eyes, while of a good size and colour, were fringed with unspectacular, mousey lashes, her nose was too sharp and too thin, which gave her rather an inquiring look, and her mouth, although nicely curved, was far too large. She was almost twenty-three, but seemed older than this, partly because she had formed the habit of screwing her pale brown hair into a severe bun, and partly because she was a quiet girl who enjoyed tranquil pursuits—not that this trait in her character had prevented her from having a great number of friends at the hospital where she had just completed her training, for although quiet, she had a sense of humour and a ready but not unkind wit.

She surveyed the scene around her now with calm eyes. Before her, straight ahead, there loomed a tree-covered hill, presumably quite inaccessible. At its foot, on either side of the village, there were roads, narrow and lonely, each disappearing around the base of the hill. She knew that her sister lived on the south-west side of the island, so it would be the road on the left—she stared at it patiently and was presently rewarded by the sight of a Landrover belting along towards the quay. It was her brother-in-law; he drew up exactly beside her, got out, embraced her with affection, flung her luggage into the Landrover, besought her to get in beside him, and almost before she had time to settle herself, had turned the car and was racing back the way he had come.

'Rotten day,' her companion volunteered. 'Good journey?'

'Yes, thanks, Tom. It seemed to go on for ever and ever, though. Are you and Rachel ready to leave?'

'Just about. It's nice of you to come, Cassandra—I hope the kids won't be too much of a handful.'

'But it's just what I wanted to do—it'll be lovely to have a month or two's break before I take my midder, and I need a change from London.'

He gave her a shrewd glance. 'Did they offer you a job?'

'As a matter of fact, they did.'

'Ward Sister?'

She went a little pink. 'Yes—Men's Medical, but if I'd taken it, I should have had to start straight away and stayed a year at least, and I might have got into a rut and not wanted to do midwifery. I think it's best to leave, don't you?'

Her companion swung the Landrover off the road on to a narrow winding lane with mountains towering to the right of them, and presently, the sight of a loch on their left. 'Yes, I think you're wise, and it's wonderful for us. You won't be lonely? The children love it, but after London…'

'I shall love it too.' Cassandra looked around her. 'It must be beautiful in the summer.' She added mildly, 'But I daresay it's pretty super at this time of year too—when it's not raining.'

'It can be gorgeous. Anyway, the house is pretty comfortable, and I suppose you've brought your knitting with you.'

'Not knitting,' she assured him gravely. 'I'm doing a firescreen in gros-point and I've brought plenty of books with me too. Besides, there won't be all that time to spare, will there, not with Penny and Andrew for company. How's their school?'

'Excellent. Small, but the teaching is first class.'

'And the book?'

'Finished. Here we are.'

The road was running beside the loch now, pushed there by the mountains, and then the loch ended abruptly, leaving only a wild, narrow river in its place, which in its turn opened suddenly into a much larger loch and gave Cassandra her first glimpse of her future home for the next few weeks. The village was very small and scattered, with an austere church in its centre and a few fishing boats drawn up beside the jetty. Its one street contained a single shop, but Cassandra had no chance to do more than glance at it as Tom drove on, out of the village and along a track running up the hillside. He stopped after a half mile, however, turned in through a wide gate and pulled up before a well-built house with a grey slate roof and whitewashed walls. The door was flung open as Cassandra prepared to get out and the two children and their mother came out to meet her.

Rachel was ten years older than her sister and had more than her fair share of good looks, although it was easy to see that they were sisters. She hugged Cassandra with real delight and then held her away to have a good look at her.

'Lovely to see you,' she said. 'You look as though you could do with a holiday, darling. I'm so glad you decided to leave hospital, even if it is only for a month or two—besides, it's wonderful for us to be able to get away on our own for a few weeks—these brats can't wait to see us go.' She smiled at the two children with her and they laughed back at her little joke. They didn't mind in the least being left with their Aunt Cassandra—she was clever at making things and talked to them as though they were intelligent people and not half-witted kids. Andrew, her nephew, offered a rather grubby hand and grinned at her, but Penny, who was only five, threw herself at her favourite aunt and hugged her.

Indoors there was a roaring fire in the sitting-room. Cassandra had her wet coat taken from her, was invited to take off her boots and her head-scarf, and sat before the blaze while her sister went to the kitchen to fetch the coffee.

'Anyone interesting on the boat?' Rachel inquired when she returned.

Cassandra wriggled her toes in the pleasant warmth. 'No, I don't think so—there weren't many people on board and they all melted away. You're a long way away from everywhere, aren't you?'

Rachel passed her a brimming mug. 'Miles,' she agreed comfortably. 'But the village is nice; you'll be absorbed into it in no time at all. You've got the Landrover. You're not nervous of being alone at night, are you? You've no need to be.'

'I'm not—you can't think how marvellous it's going to be, going to sleep in peace and quiet without traffic tearing past the windows all night.'

'She was offered a Sister's post,' Tom told his wife as he sat down, and Rachel exclaimed: 'Cassy, how marvellous for you—you didn't refuse it because of us, did you?' She sounded concerned.

Cassandra shook her head. 'Of course not. I was telling Tom, if I had taken it, I should have got into a rut and stayed for ever and ever. Now I'm free to take my midder when I want. I've enough money to tide me over for a bit—besides, you've given me much more than I shall ever need.' She broke off. 'What do you do when you want to shop—I mean really shop?'

Rachel laughed. 'You park the kids with Mrs MacDonnell, the schoolteacher. She'll take them home for their dinner and you collect them when you get back from Oban. You can take the Landrover to the ferry and leave it near the quay and collect it on your way back—I've been doing that every few weeks.'

'Well,' said Cassandra, 'I don't suppose I shall want to go at all—I just wanted to know.'

Andrew, sitting beside her, said suddenly, 'There's

a village shop—it's super, you can buy anything there.'

His aunt gave him an understanding look. 'Toffee?' she suggested. 'Crayons, pen-knives, balls of string and those awful things that change colour when you suck them? I've no doubt we shall do very well. What time do you leave?' She turned to her brother-in-law.

'Tomorrow afternoon. We'll all go to the ferry and you can drive the kids back afterwards, Cassy. Our plane leaves Glasgow in the evening—we'll spend the night in London and go on to Greece in the morning.' He stretched luxuriously. 'Six weeks' holiday!' he purred. 'I can hardly believe it!'

'You deserve it,' remarked his wife. 'This book's been a bit of a grind, hasn't it?'

He nodded. 'But at least I've got the Roman Empire out of my system for ever. I always wanted to write about it, but never again—too much research. The next one will be a modern novel. I daresay I'll get some ideas for it while we're away.'

Rachel groaned. 'Which means you'll write all day and I'll have to sit and knit.'

'I didn't know you could,' observed Cassandra.

'I can't, that's what makes it so difficult.'

Tom laughed. 'My poor darling, I promise you I'll only take notes—very brief ones.' He got up from his chair. 'How about taking Cassandra up to her room?'

They all trooped upstairs, Tom ahead with the lug-

gage, the girls arm in arm and the children darting
from side to side and getting in everyone's way. Her
bedroom was in the front of the house with a view
of the sea, and if she craned her neck out of the
window, the mountains as well. It was most comfortably furnished and pleasantly warm, with cheerful carpeting to match the cherry red curtains and
bedspread. She began to unpack with everyone sitting around watching her as she handed out the small
presents she had brought with her. They had been
difficult to choose because she hadn't a great deal of
money and Tom was able to give Rachel and the
children almost everything they could want. All the
same, everyone exclaimed delightedly over their gifts
and finally Rachel produced one for Cassandra—a
thick hand-knitted Arran sweater. 'To wear around,'
she explained. 'I expect you've got some thick skirts
and slacks with you—the children are great walkers
and so are you, aren't you? And there's nothing
much else you can wear here. Have you got some
stout shoes?'

For answer Cassandra unearthed a sturdy pair from
her case. 'And my boots, and I suppose I can borrow
someone's Wellies.'

They all trooped downstairs then and had lunch,
then did the last-minute packing while Mrs Todd,
who came in to help, did the washing-up.

The rain had ceased by the time they had finished
and Cassandra changed into her new sweater and a
pair of slacks, tied a scarf over her hair, and joined

her relations for a walk. They went first to the village, where she made the acquaintance of Mrs MacGill, who owned the shop, and on the way out of it, the pastor, an almost middle-aged man, very thin and stooping, with hair combed tidily over the bald patch on the top of his head, and thick glasses. He shook hands with Cassandra, expressed himself delighted to make her acquaintance and hoped that she would go to the Manse one day and take tea with himself and his sister. He added, a little sternly, that he would see her in church on the following Sunday, and walked away rather abruptly.

They were well clear of the village, going along a rough track winding up the wooded hillside, when Tom observed, 'You've made a hit, Cassy—I've never known old John Campbell issue an invitation to anyone until at least a month after he's met them.'

'Will you marry him?' inquired Penny. 'I don't think I should like that, Aunt Cassandra.'

'No, well—I don't think I should myself, poppet, and as I don't suppose there's the slightest possibility of that happening, I think I'll forget about it and concentrate on a prince in shining armour.'

'So awkward,' murmured Rachel, 'the armour, I mean. However did they manage to give a girl a good hug, do you suppose?'

This interesting point held everybody's attention for some time, it certainly lasted until they had reached the brow of the hill where they were met by a splendid wind and a vast expanse of grey sea and sky.

'No view at all,' said Tom in disgust, 'and it looks like bad weather. We'd better get back, I think. We can go down the other path.'

They got home before the rain, glowing from walking fast, and the sitting-room looked very inviting as they crowded in. They made toast and ate a great deal of cake as well, and drank quantities of tea from an enormous teapot. It was nice, Cassandra reflected, that Rachel had never allowed Tom's success and money to interfere with the happy home life she had achieved for them all. The house was roomy, well furnished and there was every comfort one could reasonably wish for, but the children weren't spoilt; there was no obvious luxury, although she knew that Rachel could have anything she wanted and more besides.

She looked with affection at her sister, sitting curled up in one of the armchairs. She didn't look her age; her pretty face was smooth and happy and contented—she was a dear; since their parents had died, she had, in the nicest possible way, looked after Cassandra, inviting her for holidays when they went abroad, giving her the pretty things she couldn't quite afford to buy for herself, but only at birthdays and Christmas, so that Cassandra had never felt patronized. She had even contrived several meetings with young men when she and Tom had been living in London, so that Cassandra should have the opportunity of making their acquaintance. But this hadn't been entirely successful; there were too many pretty girls around for the young men in question to waste more than a polite few minutes with her. Perhaps if she could have been a sparkling talker she might have achieved something, but she wasn't, and she had never felt quite at ease with them.

She bit into another slice of cake, thinking how fortunate it was that she could repay Rachel and Tom a little for their kindness by minding the children while they took a holiday. They had wanted to go away together for some time, she knew, but neither of them would consider it unless the children could be looked after by someone they trusted. There were no grandparents now, and Tom's sister, who lived in London, was heartily disliked by his children—that only left herself, and she had been able to say yes when Rachel had written and asked tentatively if there was any chance of her having a holiday and if so, could she bear to spend it looking after her nephew and niece. She had written back at once and offered to stay as long as they wanted her to, glad of the opportunity to get away from hospital life for a little while.

She loved her work, but a change was good for everyone and for the last six months, while she had been working in theatre, she had fancied herself in love with the young Surgical Registrar, who unfortunately, had barely noticed her—an unrewarding experience which she had the sense to know would get

her nowhere. Up here, on this remote island, leading
a totally different life, she would forget him quickly
enough. She sighed, and Rachel asked anxiously,
'You won't miss London, darling?'

'Me? No. Just think of it, six weeks of this— I
shall read and sew and cook and discipline the
kids...'

A remark which was greeted with delighted gig-
gles from the children, because the idea of their be-
loved Aunt Cassandra disciplining anyone or, for that
matter, being even faintly stern, was just too funny
for words. They were still giggling as they led her
away upstairs, where presently a furious uproar sig-
nified the fact that they were having their bedtime
baths.

The weather had changed when Cassandra got up
the next morning; the sun shone from a chilly blue
sky, turning the sea to a turbulent green and the hills
to yellow and red and brown, and in the distance the
snowcapped mountains looked as though they had
been painted against the horizon. The village was
bright and cosy in the sunshine, its roofs and white
walls sparkling, its windows gleaming. The sun was
still shining as she drove back from the ferry in the
afternoon with the two quiet and rather tearful children. The sky was paler now and already dim around
its edges where the dusk was creeping in. Cassandra
kept up a flow of cheerful conversation all the way
home and as she swung the Landrover up the short
track to the house, she asked:

'How about a walk before tea? Just a short one—
Bob needs some exercise and so do I. I'd love to go
a little way up the hill behind the house.'

They set off presently, climbing steadily up the
path which wound through the trees. It was sheltered
from the wind and surprisingly quiet.

'There'll be mice here,' said Cassandra, 'and rab-
bits and an owl or two, I daresay, and any number
of birds—I wish I knew their names. There's a squirrel.'

They stood still and watched the creature dart up
a tree and Bob, the elderly Labrador, who had grown
portly with his advancing years, sat down.

'Draw him when we get home,' Penny begged her.

'Certainly, my dear, if you would like that.' Her
aunt smiled fondly at her and added briskly, 'Shall
we go to that bend in the path and then go back for
tea?'

There was a gap in the trees at the path's turn; it
afforded an excellent view of the hill above them,
and the sun, gleaming faintly now, shone on something near its summit, in amongst the trees. Cassandra, staring hard, saw that it was a window and what
was more, there was a chimney besides, with smoke
wreathing above it.

'A house!' she exclaimed. 'Whoever lives there?
Why, it's miles away from the village.'

For the first time since they had parted from their
parents, the children perked up.

'That's Ogre's Relish,' Andrew informed her importantly, and waited confidently for her reply, for unlike other, sillier aunts, she could be depended upon to give the right answers.

'What an extremely clever name,' said Cassandra. 'Do tell.'

She watched his little chest swell with pride. 'I thought of it—Penny helped,' he added. 'There's a man lives there, and one day I heard Mrs Todd telling Mrs MacGill that he relished his peace and quiet, and of course he's an ogre because no one's ever seen him.'

His aunt nodded her complete understanding. 'Of course. Does he live alone?'

Penny answered her. 'There's another man there too—he's old, and he comes to the shop sometimes and buys things, but he hardly ever speaks and Mrs MacGill says he only buys enough to keep body and soul together. Are ogres poor, Aunt Cassandra?'

'This one sounds as though he might be.'

'He can't see.'

Cassandra stopped to look at her small niece. 'My darling, are you sure? I mean, not see at all?'

Andrew chipped in: 'We don't know, but I heard Daddy tell Mummy, he said. "He can't see, poor beggar." That means,' he explained, just in case his aunt hadn't quite grasped the point, 'that he's not got any money—not if he's a beggar.'

Cassandra nodded; it seemed hardly the time to start a dull explanation about figures of speech, and even if the poor ogre had enough to live on, it seemed a dreary enough existence. She turned her back on the gap, shivering a little. 'Let's go home,' she said.

She took the children down to the village school the next morning and then went back to give Mrs Todd a hand in the house; but Mrs Todd assured her that she needed no help, so she retired to the kitchen and set about preparing their midday dinner. There was more than enough to choose from; she delved into the deep-freeze and settled on lamb chops and by way of afters she made a queen of puddings, adding homemade strawberry jam with a lavish hand and wondering as she did so if the poor ogre really had enough to eat. She found herself thinking about him as she worked; one day soon, while the children were at school, she would climb the path behind the house and call on him—he might be glad of a visitor, but perhaps he didn't like callers, so it might be a good idea to walk up the hill and spy out the land first. Still busy with her thoughts, she started on a cake for tea, for the chocolate one had been demolished for all but two slices. She made the coffee, called to Mrs Todd to join her and they sat together in the kitchen, consuming the rest of the cake between them. Mrs Todd, Cassandra discovered, was a perfect fount of knowledge; she was told all about the pastor and the pastor's sister, who according to her companion, was a proper old termagant. 'No wonder the puir man has never taken a wife,' she observed.

'Who'd want to with him, knowing she's landed with his sister too?'

Cassandra, her mouth full of cake, agreed fervently, 'And the man who lives in the cottage behind us on the hill?' she wanted to know casually.

'Och, him. Now, there's a tale I could tell ye...'

And never to be told, for the doorbell rang at just that moment. It was the lad from a neighbouring farm who brought the eggs each week; he had to be paid and given a cup of coffee, too, and by the time he had gone again Mrs Todd had no time left to talk. She still had to do the kitchen, she told Cassandra rather severely, and perhaps Miss Cassandra would like to go to the sitting-room or take a walk?

It was almost time to fetch the children from school; she chose to go for a walk, going the long way round to the school and calling in at the shop to buy stamps—Rachel would expect letters.

During their dinner Rachel telephoned; they were on the point of catching their flight to Athens, she told them, talking to each of them in turn and then making way for Tom, who promised that they would telephone that evening. Cassandra, who had expected the children to be tearful, was agreeably surprised to find that although they were excited to hear from their parents, they showed no signs of being unhappy. Just in case they were, she promised, rather rashly that they would play cards that evening.

The first few days went quickly and she enjoyed them; she missed the busy hospital life and the urgent work in theatre, on the other hand it was delightful to have time to read and sew and knit. Besides, she enjoyed cooking; she found a cook book and between the three of them, they chose something different each day, very much influenced by the colourful illustrations of dishes with exotic names and an enormous number of ingredients. They made toffee too and went for long rambles, so that it was almost a week before Cassandra had the opportunity of going to the cottage on the hill. The children had been invited to a birthday party in the village, a protracted affair which would last well into the evening. She had walked down with them just after two o'clock on the Saturday afternoon and seen them safely into the cottage where the party was to be held and then, her mind made up, went back through the village. She had almost reached the track leading to her sister's house, when John Campbell came out of the manse front door.

She stopped because he had called a greeting as she went past and it would have been rude not to have stopped, and he quite obviously wanted to talk. They stood together, chatting about nothing in particular for five minutes or more until she said: 'Well, I'll be getting along...'

'I wondered if you would care to come to tea—today, perhaps?' he smiled at her. 'My sister would like to meet you.'

Cassandra, normally a truthful girl, lied briskly, 'I'm so sorry, I promised Rachel that I would do some telephoning for her this afternoon—family, you know—she hadn't time before she went. Besides, I've a simply enormous wash waiting in the machine.' She smiled at him kindly, quite unrepentant about the fibbing, because she was determined that she would climb the hill and take a nearer look at Ogre's Relish—and nothing was going to stop her.

It was further away than she had thought and the path became steeper as she went. It petered out at length in a small clearing from which several smaller paths wound themselves away into the trees all around her. She could see no sign of the cottage now and it took her a few moments to decide which path to take. The wrong one, as it turned out, for it led to a small enclosed patch of wild grass and thistles and heather, so she went back again and this time chose the path opposite, pausing to look about her as she went. All the same, she was taken completely by surprise when it turned a corner and opened directly into a quite large garden, very tidy and nicely sheltered by the trees. A path led to the cottage front door, set sturdily between two small windows with another two beneath its slate roof. She looked around her; the place seemed to be deserted, so perhaps it wasn't the right one. She crossed the grass with the idea of peering in through one of its windows and then let out a small gasp when a voice from behind her said:

'You're trespassing, my good woman.'

The ogre! She forced herself to turn round slowly,

filled with a ridiculous, childish fear which was instantly dispelled when she saw the dark glasses and the stick. For an ogre, she thought idiotically, he was remarkably handsome; tall and broad-shouldered, with dark hair greying at the temples, the dark glasses bridging a long straight nose beneath thick brows. His mouth was well shaped and firm too, although at the moment it was drawn down in a faint sneer. Probably, she told herself with her usual good sense, she would sneer too if she had to wear dark glasses and carry a stick... She found her tongue: 'Good afternoon. I'm sorry if I'm trespassing—I didn't mean to come into your garden, it was unexpected...'

The dark glasses glared at her. 'Only to spy out the land, perhaps?'

Cassandra flushed. 'Well, yes—at least, you see, I knew you lived here—the children told me about you.'

'Indeed?' The dark glasses bored a hole through her, the voice was icy. 'And should I be flattered?'

'Why?' she asked matter-of-factly, and went on: 'The children—my nephew and niece, were telling me.'

'I'm all agog,' he said nastily.

'Well, they're only small children and imaginative—they call this cottage Ogre's Relish.'

His lips twitched. 'So I am an ogre?'

'No, not really. They've heard about you and they made up stories.'

'Really?' His voice was cold and she gave him an apprehensive look and said uneasily: 'You're not offended?'

'What does it matter to you?' he wanted to know coolly. 'Don't let me keep you.'

He might not be an ogre, but certainly he had the disposition of one! Cassandra retreated down the path and paused to ask: 'Can you see at all?' knowing that it was unpardonable of her to ask, but wanting very much to know. He didn't bother to answer her and she took another step away from him, then stopped again because another man, elderly this time and as dark as the ogre, had come round the corner of the cottage. He had his sweater sleeves rolled up and the first thing Cassandra's sharp eyes saw were the numbers tattooed on his arm, between his wrist and his elbow. She knew what they meant—he had been in a concentration camp. He had the face of an old hawk and looked decidedly surly, but all the same she wished him a good afternoon and he gave a surprised, reluctant reply. Still more surprising, however, was the fact that the man in the dark glasses spoke. 'This is Jan, my good friend—he can do everything except make cakes.' He smiled a little. 'He speaks excellent English and Polish, if you should have a knowledge of that language, but don't on any account address him in German; he dislikes that, for his own very good reasons.'

Cassandra said briefly: 'I can't speak anything but English and school French.' She put out her hand.

'How do you do, Jan?' and shook his hand, careful not to look at the tattooed numbers. 'I daresay I shall see you some time in the shop, shan't I?' She smiled and saw the faint reflection in his own face. She wished the ogre would smile too—he would look very nice then—if he ever did, but he seemed a bitter man, which was natural enough. She wondered how he had come to lose his sight in the first place and longed to ask him, although she knew that to be impossible. She wished him a pleasant good-bye which he answered with the briefest of nods in her direction, and started back down the path. She was almost home when she remembered that he had never answered her question as to whether he could see at all.

The next day being Sunday, she took the children to church, a bare whitewashed building, filled to capacity, and after the service, when she paused at the door to wish Mr Campbell a good morning, she was bidden to wait a few moments so that she might meet Miss Campbell, a treat she wasn't particularly anxious to experience. The lady, when she came, was exactly as Cassandra had pictured her, only more so; she was younger than her brother, with a determined chin and cold blue eyes which examined Cassandra's London-bought hat with suspicion and then raked her face, looking for signs of the frivolity the owner of such a hat would be sure to possess. But there was nothing frivolous about Cassandra's face; Miss Campbell sighed with vexation—she had already

heard far too much about this young woman from
London from her brother, who, at his age, should
know better, and now she had seen for herself that
there were none of the more regrettable aspects of
the modern world visible in the girl—only the hat.
She would have her to tea, she decided, and show
her up, with her usual skill, before her brother, and
Cassandra, while unaware of these thoughts, sensed
that she wasn't liked—well, she didn't like Miss
Campbell either. She murmured noncommittally over
the invitation to tea and made a polite escape with
the murmured excuse that she had the Sunday dinner
to see to.

Out of hearing, she was immediately attacked by
her two small companions.

'But you got the dinner ready before we came out,
Aunt Cassandra,' Andrew pointed out.

'You said...' began Penny.

'Yes, my dears, I know. I told a fib, didn't I? I'm
very sorry, but you see I couldn't think of anything
else to say, and I didn't want to go back to the
Manse, and I believe Mr Campbell was on the point
of asking us.'

This sensible way out of an awkward situation was
immediately sanctioned, although Andrew asked
doubtfully, 'But you don't usually fib, Aunt Cassandra, do you?'

And she, in some ways as young as her companions, crossed her fingers as she assured him that no,
she did her best not to.

She thought about the ogre quite a lot during the next few days, and when she met Jan in the village shop and saw the meagre groceries he was buying, she went home, baked a large fruit cake and that same afternoon, after the children had gone back to school, climbed the path behind the house once more.

Probably she would get the cake thrown at her, but at least she had to try; the thought of the two men living in a kind of exile without enough to eat and with no hope of a home-made cake for their teas touched her heart—and perhaps this time the ogre would be more friendly. She had no wish to pry, she knew how difficult it was for anyone to reconcile themselves to blindness, especially when they were young—and he was still young, she guessed about thirty-five.

This time she walked boldly up the path and knocked on the door, and was rewarded by the ogre's voice bidding her to go in and shut the door behind her. It led directly into the sitting-room, small and cosy and extremely untidy, but none the less clean. Cassandra paused just inside the door and before she could speak, the man in the dark glasses said: 'It's you again.'

'Oh, you can see—I'm so glad!' said Cassandra, her plain face illuminated by delight.

'We don't have so many visitors that I can't make a shrewd guess as to who it is. Besides, Dioressence isn't so difficult to recognize—I don't imagine that there are many women in the village who wear it.' The dark glasses were turned in her direction. 'Why have you come? Did I invite you?'

A bad beginning, she had to admit. 'No—but I was in the shop this morning and Jan was there and—and…' She paused, not knowing how to say it without hurting his pride, of which she had no doubt he had far too much. 'Well, I thought you might like a cake, as you said Jan couldn't make cakes—it's only a fruit one, but if you put it into a tin it will keep for days.'

She was still standing by the door and she couldn't see his face very well, for he was sitting by the fire in a large armchair, half turned from her. He said quietly: 'Will you sit down? I'm afraid we aren't very tidy, but move anything you have to,' and when she had done so, still clutching the cake, he went on: 'You're kind. We don't encourage visitors, you know—there's no point. I'm only here for a few weeks and they are almost over.'

'You'll go home?'

'Yes.'

'I don't think you're English—or Scottish—and you can't be German because if you were Jan wouldn't be with you.'

His smile mocked her. 'Intelligent as well as beautiful,' he remarked silkily.

'If you didn't have to wear those glasses you would see that I am rather a plain girl.'

'Indeed? In which case we must allow my dark glasses to have some advantage after all.'

She went a painful scarlet. In a voice throbbing with self-restraint, she said: 'That was really rather rude.'

The mouth beneath the dark glasses sneered. 'Yes, but you asked for it, young woman.'

She got to her feet, laid the cake carefully down on the table and said in a sensible voice: 'Yes, I did, didn't I? I shall know better next time, if ever there is a next time. I came because I thought you might be lonely, but I see now that I've been officious and I expect you find me a prig as well. I'm sorry.' She was at the door, she opened it, said good-bye and was through it and away down the path with such speed that she didn't hear his sharp exclamation.

She had put the children to bed and was sitting with her gros-point in her lap, thinking about her afternoon visit and its awful failure, when there was a knock on the door. It was Jan, and when she invited him in, he shook his head and said: 'I'm not to stop, miss. Mr van Manfeld sent me to ask if you would go and see him again—tomorrow, perhaps? He wishes to talk to you.'

Cassandra felt an instant pleasure, which in the face of her recent reception at the cottage, was ridiculous. She said cautiously, 'Oh, I can't possibly come tomorrow, or the day after that—let me see…' she frowned over mythical engagements, 'perhaps Friday afternoon.'

'Not tomorrow?' inquired Jan, disappointed.

She shook her head. 'No, I'm afraid it's quite impossible. I'll come on Friday. Would you like a cup of coffee before you go?'

He gave her a suspicious look. 'No—no, thank you, miss. I was to say that the cake was very good. I'll be going.'

They wished each other good night and she shut the door upon him and stood leaning against it, wondering why the ogre should want to see her again. He hadn't liked her, had he? he had said so, not in so many words, perhaps—all the same...perhaps it was the cake. She went back to her embroidery, her mind already busy with the making of another cake, and possibly an apple pie. Her pastry was excellent, and men liked pies.

CHAPTER TWO

CASSANDRA climbed the hill path on Friday afternoon, carrying a basket this time and wrapped against the fine rain and boisterous wind in an elderly anorak of Rachel's, and this time when she knocked on the door, Jan opened it for her and ushered her inside as Mr van Manfeld rose from his seat by the fire to greet her. She hadn't quite expected that, and although he didn't smile at least his face wore a look of polite welcome. She stared at the dark glasses and wondered what colour the eyes they concealed would be, then, rather belatedly, wished him a good afternoon. 'I've brought another cake, a chocolate one, and an apple pie—I was making one for us and it seemed silly not to...'

She stopped because it was a stupid sort of speech anyway, but someone had to say something. Jan had nodded at her and disappeared through a door leading presumably to the kitchen, and Mr van Manfeld took so long to say anything that she had to quell a desire to put her basket on the table and go away again.

'I didn't think that you would come,' said her host at length. 'Why did you?'

'Well, you asked me, and I said I would—and besides, I thought you might be glad of another cake.'

He smiled then and his whole face changed. 'I have a vile temper,' he informed her, 'and I have allowed it to get out of hand—I hope you will forgive me for my rudeness.'

Cassandra, ever practical, was taking off her anorak and went to hang it behind the door. 'Yes, of course, and you're not as rude as all that. The village…'

'Discuss me? Naturally. But I came here to get away from people. Will you sit down?'

She took the chair opposite his and tried not to stare at the glasses; instead she picked up a small ginger kitten sitting before the fire, and put it on her lap. 'You said you were going home soon—so I suppose you came here to convalesce or wait for results.'

The eyebrows rose. 'Is that a guess?' and when she said yes, he went on:

'I'm awaiting results. There is a good chance that my blindness isn't permanent, what sight I have has already much improved, but I depend on my eyes for my work—I'm a surgeon.' He added impatiently, 'But I can't expect you to understand.'

'Yes, you can. I'm a nurse, you see, and I've just done six months in theatre and I've watched the surgeons at work. Is it an optic nerve injury?'

'Yes. A paralysis which is slowly righting itself, I hope.' He spoke curtly and without any wish to continue the subject, something which became apparent when he went on: 'I asked you to come so that I might apologize to you. I was abominably rude and you were most forbearing. I should warn you that I frequently lose my temper.'

The silence after this frank statement became rather long. Cassandra sat, wondering if she was supposed to go, or was she to stay a little while, even have tea? She was on the point of making some remark about getting back when Jan came in from the kitchen. To her disappointment he was empty-handed; she had, after all, come quite a long way and at Mr van Manfeld's request. Whatever better feeling had caused him to invite her had cooled. She got up and offered Jan the basket. 'If you wouldn't mind putting these in the kitchen,' she asked, and he nodded without looking at her and put out a stringy arm upon which the hideous tattoo stood out sharply.

She was normally a composed girl, not given to impulsive actions, but now she put out her hand and touched his arm gently and said: 'Jan, I'm so sorry about this—I wanted to tell you.'

Jan looked at her then; his eyes were black and she thought for a moment that he was very angry, but he wasn't. He smiled and patted her hand and said: 'Thank you, miss.' He might have said more, but Mr van Manfeld gave a short mocking laugh.

'Spare me a mawkish scene!' he begged nastily. 'And should you not be going back to your charges, Miss...?'

'Darling,' Cassandra told him crisply, 'and don't dare to be funny about it!'

'I'm never funny,' he assured her, 'and if it is your inappropriate name to which you refer, I can think of nothing more unsuitable. There is nothing darling about you—you invade my privacy without so much as a by-your-leave, you subject me to your quite unnecessary sentiment, and you assure me that you are not pretty. I really think you should go.' His voice was cool, faintly amused, and mocking.

Cassandra stared at the dark glasses. The mouth below them was pulled down into a half smile which was fast becoming a sneer—and he had smiled so nicely. She sighed. 'I'm not surprised that the children call you an ogre,' she informed him tartly, 'because you are a most ill-mannered man, which is a pity, because I expect you're quite nice really.'

The glasses glared. 'Oh, go away!' he snapped, and got up from his chair. He looked very large and almost menacing. 'God's teeth,' he ground out savagely, 'what have...'

Cassandra's firm chin went up in the air. 'What a shocking remark to make!' but he didn't allow her to finish.

'Don't be so prissy,' he advised her sourly, 'I'm no mealy-mouthed parson.'

She allowed herself a moment's comparison of Mr Campbell and the man before her and was surprised to find that Mr Campbell came off second best. 'I'm sure he's a very good man and kind.'

'Meaning that I'm not? As though I care a damn
what you think, my pious Miss Darling—going to
church in your best hat and probably making the reverend's heart flutter to boot. You sound just his sort.'

'I'm not anyone's sort, Mr van Manfeld.' She
picked up her empty basket and went to the door,
her voice coming loud and rather wobbly. 'It's a
good thing you can't see me, because I'm extremely
angry.'

His voice followed her, still sour. 'But I can see
you after a fashion. It's true you're dark blue and
very fuzzy round the edges, but since you assure me
that you're a plain girl, I don't really see that it matters, do you?'

Cassandra ground her teeth without answering this
piece of rudeness and banged the door regrettably
hard as she went out.

There was a note the next day, presumably delivered
by hand while she had been out. It was typed and
signed rather crookedly with the initials B. van M. It
begged her pardon and asked her to go to the cottage
and stay for tea. She read it several times, then tore
it up. There was another note the following day; it
was waiting for her when she got back from church
with the children, and she tore that one up too and
hurried to get their dinner because, having run out of
excuses, she had accepted Miss Campbell's invitation to tea that afternoon, and she was to take Andrew and Penny with her. She had, she told herself

firmly, no intention of going anywhere near the ogre
ever again. She found the idea distressing.

Tea at the Manse was run on strictly conventional
lines. Everyone sat round the drawing-room eating
slippery sandwiches and crumbling cake from plates
which weren't quite big enough. The children,
coaxed into exemplary behaviour, sat like two small
statues, making despairing efforts to catch the
crumbs before they reached the floor, and Cassandra,
seated with her hostess on a remarkably hard sofa,
watched them with sympathy. It was a relief when
the clock struck five and she was able to say that
they should be going home before the dusk de-
scended. 'And anyway,' she went on politely, 'you
will want to get ready for church, I expect.'

She had no ready reply when her host, despite the
speaking look his sister gave him, professed himself
ready to accompany them to their door.

'There's no need,' cried Cassandra, who even if
he hadn't, had seen the look and didn't want his company anyway. 'It's only ten minutes' walk, and it's
not dark yet.'

Which made it worse, because the pastor pointed
out that he couldn't possibly allow a young and
pretty woman to go that distance, especially with the
children, he added. It made it sound as though the
village were some vice-ridden haunt full of desperate
characters with flick-knives waiting at every corner.
Cassandra suppressed a giggle and they set off sedately, each with a child holding a hand. At the door

she felt bound to ask him in, and was quite downcast when he accepted.

He didn't stay long, although she had the impression that he would have done so if time hadn't been pressing. She saw him to the door, murmuring politely about the tea-party, and suggesting vaguely that he and his sister might care to take tea with them at some future date. When he had gone, Andrew rounded on her. 'Aunt Cassandra, how could you? Ask him to tea, I mean. He's all right, I suppose, but Miss Campbell's always so cross. Did you hear her telling Penny off because she made crumbs, and she couldn't help it.'

Cassandra led the way to the kitchen. 'Darlings, I know. I made crumbs too, but you see it would be so rude not to invite them back. But if they come on a Sunday they have to be back by six o'clock—earlier—so it wouldn't be too bad.'

She opened the fridge and took out some milk, and Andrew, standing beside her, said: 'He fancies you, Aunt Cassandra.'

She gave him a look of horror. 'Andrew, you're making it up! He couldn't—you mustn't make remarks like that,' she rebuked him. 'You're only repeating something you've heard.'

He mistook her meaning. 'That's right. I heard someone in the shop yesterday—that's what they said.' He was speaking the truth; Cassandra said lightly: 'Oh, gossip, darling, you shouldn't listen to

that, no one ever means it. Now, supper—I planned
a rather nice one.'

The pastor wasn't mentioned again, for after supper they played Monopoly until bedtime, which left
no time to talk. It was later, when she was sitting in
the quiet house, writing to Rachel, that Cassandra
paused to worry about Andrew's remark. Mr Campbell was a very nice man, she had no doubt, but
definitely not her cup of tea. Besides, she didn't like
his sister. She would do her best to avoid him as
much as possible, though how to do that in a village
of such a small size was going to be a problem. She
brightened at the thought that it was only just over a
month until she would be gone and the problem
would solve itself, but her relief was tempered by a
very real regret that she would never see Mr van
Manfeld again; even in a rage he was interesting
company, and surely, sometimes he was good-
tempered. It would be nice to know, but she doubted
if she ever would.

She had the opportunity of doing so the very next
day. She had taken the children back to school after
their dinner and was sitting on the floor before the
fire with the animals, doing nothing, when the front
door bell rang.

Mr van Manfeld stood outside with Jan beside
him. He wore a sheepskin jacket which made him
truly vast, so that Jan, similarly clad, looked like his
very thin shadow. The ogre said politely: 'Good afternoon, Miss Darling. I sent you two notes; you

didn't reply to them. We came to visit you yesterday afternoon, but you were not home. Taking tea with the reverend, so the village tells Jan.'

'Come inside,' said Cassandra in a no-nonsense voice. 'Coming all this way—you must be mad! You can't possibly see where you're going...' She stopped and bit her lip because her choice of words hadn't been too happy.

'Jan is my sight.' He had followed her into the hall with Jan close behind. 'I must own, my dear girl, that you are the only person I have met since my accident who hasn't cried crocodile's tears over me or wanted to lead me around like a dumb animal. I find it refreshing.' He towered over her, standing in the centre of the spacious hall. 'Can you imagine what it is like to be without sight?'

She returned the blank stare of the dark glasses steadily. 'I think so—a kind of little hell. But you're going to see again; you know far better than I do that if there's any sight left after an optic nerve injury, it's more likely to improve than worsen. Come into the sitting-room.'

She didn't attempt to show him where the chairs were; Jan had taken his jacket, now he guided him unobtrusively to one of the armchairs by the fire and at Cassandra's smiling invitation, took one close by.

'Why have you come?' she wanted to know, and sat down on the floor again with Bob and the cats.

Mr van Manfeld crossed one long leg over the other. 'Another thing I like about you, dear Miss

Darling, is your direct approach. I came because I wanted to see you again—er—figuratively speaking, of course. I am selfish, full of self-pity and evil-tempered, but I enjoy your company, therefore I force myself—and Jan—upon you, since you aren't civil enough to answer my notes.'

'Civil!' Cassandra's voice was shrill with annoyance. 'Whatever next—when I took the trouble to walk up to your cottage on Friday and you didn't so much as offer me a cup of tea...'

'Tea?' interrupted Mr van Manfeld. 'That would be delightful. I was only saying to Jan that perhaps a little female society might do us both good.'

'How right you are!' exploded Cassandra. 'But don't count on me being the female.'

He had stretched out in his chair and one of the cats had got on to his knee. He was stroking her with a large square hand—a surgeon's hand. 'But you are very female, Miss Darling. You are as bold as a lion and just as rude as I am when occasion demands. Besides, Jan and I find your cakes delicious. Do you suppose we might enter into an uneasy friendship?'

She had to laugh. She had never met anyone like him before; she wondered what he was really like behind that façade he had built up—a façade to protect him from pity. She wondered for the hundredth time what kind of accident he had had. She got up and went and stood in front of him and held out her hand. 'All right,' she said, 'an uneasy friendship, but don't expect me to be a doormat for you to wipe your rages on, because I won't.'

He shook her hand gravely, 'I think you are hoaxing me,' he remarked. 'Only a pretty girl would speak with so much confidence. I find it an incentive to regain my sight as quickly as possible.'

'No,' she declared positively, 'you mustn't think that, because I'm plain—I told you so.' She appealed to Jan: 'I am, aren't I?'

The black eyes were amused. 'I have described you to Mijnheer, miss, so there is no need for me to do so again.'

'There, you see?' she inquired of the ogre, who said instantly and with gentle blandness: 'No, I don't see, but I have great faith in Jan.'

'Oh, I am sorry,' said Cassandra contritely. 'I keep forgetting, you must think me a hard-hearted, uncaring person.'

'No, I don't think that at all.' He smiled, which delighted her so much that she said at once: 'You'll stay for tea, won't you? The children will be out of school in half an hour, if you don't mind sitting here while I fetch them? I don't like them to be out alone, I know it's not far, but I feel I should be extra careful of them. Rachel—my sister—would never forgive me.'

'We should very much like to stay, and Jan will fetch the children, won't you, Jan? They know him, I believe—they meet in the shop.'

Which remark put her in mind of the inadequate

purchases Jan made. Mr van Manfeld didn't look poor, but then there were some people who never did, preferring to starve than tell anyone. She wondered what they had eaten for their dinner, and decided to add a plate of sandwiches to the hot buttered toast and the cake. Her thoughts were interrupted by her guest inquiring the name of her training school in London, and when she had told him, he went on to ask where her home was, and when she explained that she hadn't got one, looked taken aback. 'And where do you go for your holidays?' he wanted to know.

'To Rachel and Tom, only they came up here to live a year ago so that Tom could get his book finished—it was a bit far away, but now I'm here for six weeks while they are in Greece. Besides, it's wonderful for me, because I'd planned to leave Duke's and take my midwifery.'

'When?'

'When Rachel and Tom come home.'

'Have you already applied?'

She was surprised at his interest, but perhaps he welcomed the chance to talk about something different. She answered readily enough: 'No—at least, I applied months ago and I have to let them know by the end of the month.'

'Three weeks' time.'

'Yes. You ask a lot of questions.'

'Meaning it's your turn? Well?'

'Where do you come from? You're not English,

although you speak it perfectly. I think you're Dutch.'

He inclined his head. 'You are correct, my dear Miss Darling. I come from Utrecht, or rather, that is where I do most of my work. My home is in a small town called Rhenen, on the north bank of the Rhine.'

'A pretty name—is it a pretty place?'

'I think so.'

It was apparent that she had been allowed her quota of questions. She got up, saying: 'Will Jan really not mind fetching the children? If not, I can go.' She smiled at the older man as she spoke and he got to his feet.

'I should like to go. Mijnheer?'

Mr van Manfeld nodded. 'Yes, go by all means, Jan.'

When they were alone together Cassandra made up the fire, said matter-of-factly. 'I'm going to switch on a lamp, a small one on this side of the room. Do you want to close your eyes when I do it?' and then, 'I'm going to make the tea.'

'Must you? Or is it an excuse to get away from me?'

'Why should I want to get away from you?' She sounded reasonable. 'I asked you to stay for tea. I didn't have to, you know.'

'You're heaping coals of fire, Miss Darling.'

'Well, I don't mean to,' she declared. 'Why were you so bad-tempered on Friday?' She saw the look on his face and added hastily: 'All right, you don't have to answer, and I'm not being nosey, I just wondered.'

He stirred in his chair. 'I had a visit from the man who is looking after my eyes—he's pretty good in his own line. I had hoped that he would say that I might wear different glasses—that there had been some dramatic improvement. I was disappointed, and I haven't yet acquired the patience of the blind.'

She said with quick sympathy: 'Being a surgeon makes it much harder for you, and not knowing if you will be able to go on with your work makes it even harder, doesn't it?'

He winced. 'You have a knack of touching a raw wound, dear girl, even if it is with a gentle finger.'

'I don't mean to hurt you, truly I don't. But cast your mind back, Mr van Manfeld. You were totally blind at first, weren't you? And now you can see just a little, out of focus and blurred, but you can see, so you are getting better. Can't you remember that?'

He didn't answer her and when he spoke he sounded thoughtful. 'I wish I could see your face.' He smiled, and although he couldn't see, she smiled back.

The children came tumbling into the house, excited because Jan had fetched them from school and had told them that he would be staying for tea. They came into the sitting-room, still in their outdoor clothes, and stood staring silently.

'Come and meet the ogre, my dears,' invited Cassandra cheerfully. 'His name is Mr van Manfeld and

he and Jan have come to call. His dark glasses make
it difficult for him to see, so go and stand in front of
him and shake hands.' Her practical voice made everything normal to their childish ears. They offered
hands, said how do you do in small polite voices,
and Andrew asked, disappointment colouring his
voice: 'You're not an ogre?'

'Well, no, not a storybook ogre, I'm afraid, but I
have got some very ogreish habits, and as you can
see, I am a little on the large side, though small for
an ogre—but I have got enormous feet.'

The children examined his heavy brogues with interest, demanding to know what size. Cassandra left
them to it and went to get the tea.

Jan came to help her carry in the tea things. 'We
always have it round the fire,' she explained. 'I hope
you won't mind—and we're always famished, so I
hope you'll both eat a lot.'

Which they did. She watched the plates empty and
the cake diminish, while she listened to Mr van Manfeld talking nicely to the children.

She talked to Jan at the same time, polite nothings,
although she would have liked to ask him about his
native Poland, but perhaps he didn't care to talk
about it, so to be on the safe side she talked about
the village and the country around them and listened,
after a time, with real interest to his replies, because
he knew a great deal about the island. She was telling
him about the squirrel when Penny interrupted to say:

'Aunt Cassandra drew him when we got home. She drew lots of mice too—she draws beautifully.'

She trotted off and came back presently with Cassandra's sketch book and opened it for Jan to see.

'You are talented, miss,' he said quietly, and pushed the book towards Penny. 'Take the book, if you please, to Mijnheer and tell him what is in it.'

She watched the two children, one each side of their visitor, telling him in a muddled chorus about the mice and when they had finished, he asked:

'Will you keep this book for me, and when I can see again, I should like to see it with my own eyes, although I must say yours were a very good substitute.' He closed it and got up. 'Jan, I think we must go or the animals will wonder where we are.'

'Animals?' cried Cassandra and the children.

'The kitten—you may have seen him? He came looking for a home—a fox with a broken leg, a tawny owl, a robin with a broken wing—that's all we have at the moment. They come and go.'

It was Penny who asked: 'Please may we come and see them? We won't disturb you...'

'I should be delighted if you would all come. On Saturday afternoon perhaps, when there is no school, and we will have tea, though not such a splendid one as we have had today. I will send a message.'

They all went to the door and Cassandra said: 'You will take care? It's not a very easy path—you've a torch?' and Jan nodded a little impatiently as he said good-bye and turned to go, but Mr van

Manfeld paused on the step. 'Your name is beautiful. May I call you Cassandra? I think it must suit you very well.'

The two men disappeared into the thickening dusk and Cassandra drew the children indoors and shut the winter evening out. The three of them washed up to the accompaniment of an animated discussion on their visitors. 'I like the ogre,' said Penny. 'And so do I,' added Andrew. 'Do you like him, Aunt Cassandra?'

She was forced to admit that she did, and for the first time since she had fancied herself in love with the Surgical Registrar, she regretted not having a face as charming as her name.

They were drinking their mid-morning cocoa next day when Jan rang the bell and they rushed to the door to let him in.

'Mijnheer wishes you to come this afternoon, if that is possible. He is sorry that he sent no message, but there were things…'

Presumably she was supposed to accept the 'things' as an excuse, and of course the children had no hesitation in saying that they would go immediately after their dinner. Cassandra, not wishing Mr van Manfeld to have everything all his own way, modified this statement with the promise of their arrival during the afternoon. 'And do tell Mr van Manfeld that we are pleased to come; it will mean changing our plans for the afternoon, but luckily you came before we had made final arrangements.'

Jan fixed her with an expressionless black eye, assured her that he would deliver her message, and with the promise of seeing them all again within a few hours, took himself off.

Cassandra had privately decided to arrive just before tea time, but the children had other ideas. She found herself, much against her will, climbing the path soon after two o'clock; nothing she could say would dislodge their fixed idea that the ogre could hardly wait to see them again, and the quicker they got there the better.

They had tea sitting round the big table in the comfortable kitchen, because, as Mr van Manfeld explained, it was easier than trying to squash into the sitting-room. The talk was cheerful because the children were happy. They talked about school, their friends in the village, Bob's rheumatism, and the dead mouse Penny had found on the lawn that morning. It was she who asked suddenly: 'How long do you have to wear your blinkers, Mr van Manfeld?'

Cassandra was on the point of saying something— anything—but her host forestalled her. 'I don't know,' he said with surprising mildness. 'Not very much longer, perhaps. We shall have to wait and see, shan't we? When I throw them away shall we celebrate with a party?'

The suggestion was instantly accepted by the two children, although Penny asked: 'Can't I give a party for you? I'd love to give a party—Mummy wouldn't mind, and you can be my guest and we'll have red jelly and ice cream, and Jan can come, and the kitten. Will you?'

The ogre's face was lighted by a smile which was all kindness. 'I think that's a lovely idea. I accept your kind invitation, Penny, and we'll all come, won't we, Jan?'

At last it was time to go and, on the point of going out of the house Cassandra paused to remark: 'We've spent the whole afternoon without a single cross word.'

Mr van Manfeld took her hand and held it. 'That's the effect you have upon me, Cassandra Darling.' A remark one could take whichever way one wanted; her common sense told her that he was merely addressing her by her own name and not using a term of endearment. She followed Jan and the children down the hill, wondering when she would see him again, and hoping that it would be soon.

It was sooner than she had expected and in circumstances she could not have forseen—it was, in fact, the very next morning. They had set off for a walk before church quite early, long before the church bell began to ring. They skirted the side of the hill and Cassandra, steadfastly refusing the children's suggestion that they should go first to Ogre's Relish and see if the ogre would like to accompany them, pursued her way along a little path winding itself around the foot of the hills above it. Cassandra noticed the grey clouds piling up on the horizon, and the wind, away from the shelter of the trees, blew cold. She had intended to follow the path along the loch and back the same way, but now she decided to turn off and strike inland, along the narrow rocky path over the rough turf. It followed a small wild stream which presently became a waterfall and they stopped to admire it. The ground was open now, the trees retreating on either side of them to come together again ahead of them, so that they could see nothing but pines around them.

'We have to go left at the fork,' said Cassandra, but at the fork Penny stopped. 'There's water down there, Aunt Cassandra,' she cried, 'down this other path—it's another loch, a teeny-weeny one. Please may we go a little way and look at it?'

There was no reason why they shouldn't. The path ended abruptly on a small turf platform poised above the water, still slippery from the night's rain because there was no sun there. Penny, behind Cassandra, lost her footing, knocked her off her feet and slithered with a splash into the water. It wasn't far, ten feet or so, and the water was as smooth as glass; she went in with a loud plop and Cassandra, scrambling to her feet, thought that her small niece would never come up again. She had pulled her anorak off by the time Penny's small head appeared above the water, and dived in. She wasn't a good swimmer, but Penny was very close to the edge.

The water was horribly cold. She gasped with the surprise of it as she surfaced, clutching the struggling Penny as she turned for the sloping turf at the water's edge. Bob was sitting above them, watching intently and whining softly, but of Andrew there was no sign. Probably he had gone for help; for all his seven years, he was a surprisingly sensible little boy and sturdy, and would make short work of getting back to the village.

Cassandra clutched her small niece tighter and turned her head from side to side, studying the banks. There must be a spot where it would be possible to scramble up, or at least push Penny to safety without the danger of her rolling off again. Bob, who had been whining steadily, startled her out of her thoughts by barking suddenly and she heard voices— Andrew's and…

'The ogre!' squeaked Penny, and Cassandra drowned the small voice with a shout of her own. 'Don't come any nearer!' her voice was urgent. 'There's no foothold—you mustn't…' she spluttered, swallowing water, 'you mustn't,' she repeated.

'Don't fuss, my dear young woman,' the ogre besought her, his voice clear and unhurried from the bank. There was a gentle splash as he slid into the water, feet first. Beside her in no time at all, he said: 'Penny, put your arms round my neck—you're quite safe, only wet and cold.' His voice was quiet and calm and quite unhurried and Penny did as he had bidden her without question. When she had anchored herself firmly he went on, still without any sound of urgency in his voice, 'Now tell me where the bank stands out in the water like a finger.'

Cassandra looked too and saw it first. 'It's on our right, on the other side.'

'Then that is where we must go, Cassandra. I take it you can swim? Keep beside me.'

She had no wish to do otherwise; even though he couldn't see, or not very much, his bulk was reassuring and some of his massive calm had spilled on to her. She ploughed along beside him. It was no great distance, but she was already tired from holding Penny and her arms felt like lead. It was nice to hear her companion advise her to put her feet down as he stood up himself. Incredibly the water was scarcely waist deep.

'A narrow shelf under water,' he explained as he slid Penny carefully on to the turf. 'It's the only place, the rest of it is bottomless.'

A remark calculated to hasten her own efforts to get on to dry land, which she achieved rather clumsily, helped by an undignified push from behind. He climbed out beside her, scooped up Penny and remarked:

'You'll have to lead the way—there should be some sort of path right the way round, but keep well away from the bank.'

Cassandra found the path quickly enough and with a hand on his arm guided him up to it, Penny quiet in his arms. It was cold and still under the trees. She shivered violently and asked: 'Where's Andrew?'

'I told him to go back to the cottage and warn Jan. Everything will be ready for us there.'

Jan had worked hard in the ten minutes or so he had had before their arrival. Penny was soon undressed and wrapped in a blanket, and sitting in front of the fire. Cassandra could hear the bath water running too—Andrew was in the kitchen getting tea, and Jan, without wasting more words, handed her a blanket and threw open a door.

'If you would undress, miss? I will dry your clothes as far as possible—you could have a bath after Penny, perhaps? And here is Mijnheer's dressing-gown.'

She did as she was told and fifteen minutes later went back into the kitchen where Jan told her to sit by the fire and handed her a mug of tea which he laced liberally with whisky.

'Jan—how kind you are. We're putting you to a lot of trouble and I must thank you.'

'I have done little,' he shrugged his shoulders. 'It is Mijnheer who did much.'

'I know.' She took a sip of fortified tea and found it surprisingly good. 'I haven't had a chance to see him yet, but I shall.'

The subject of their conversation appeared a few minutes later, clad in slacks and a sweater, to sit down in his chair again and demand to know if Jan had given her tea and put the whisky in it as he had ordered.

'Yes, thank you,' Cassandra answered him meekly, 'it makes me feel nice and warm.' Which remark he answered with a crack of laughter.

'You will all stay for lunch,' he told her, 'and Jan shall go home with you when your clothes are dry.'

'Oh, it's very kind of you,' she said, 'and Penny and I are very grateful to you for rescuing us. We should like to thank you.'

He smiled faintly. 'It's always a pleasure to rescue damsels in distress, but do thank me.'

Cassandra hadn't understood him, but Penny had; she got up from her place before the fire and went and flung her small arms round his neck and kissed him soundly. He put an arm round her and drew her to stand by his chair. 'More than thanked,' he remarked. 'The other cheek's waiting!'

'Well, really,' Cassandra remonstrated, 'I don't...'

'You must,' shrilled Penny, 'you must, Aunt Cassandra. You told me the other day that when you thank someone you have to do it properly or it's rude.'

Cassandra got to her feet, feeling a fool and very shy. She kissed the cheek he offered swiftly and took a step backwards, but his arm held her. 'Your hair is long,' he said quietly, and ran his hand down its length.

Jan came in with the soup then and they all fell to with a good deal of laughing and joking. The soup was excellent; Cassandra, who was a born cook, caught the flavour of sherry and the smoothness of cream—this was something out of a very expensive tin indeed, and she felt guiltier than ever. They were

busy with second helpings when Andrew asked
loudly:

'Are you a poor beggar, Mr van Manfeld? Daddy
said you were one day when he was talking to
Mummy.'

There was a horrid silence which seemed to stretch
on and on but which in reality lasted only a few
moments. Cassandra found her voice and broke it.
'He's only a little boy,' she said in a low urgent
voice. 'It was something he heard—he doesn't
know—you're not to be…'

The face her host turned to her was smooth, without expression, as was his voice, so why should she
feel so strongly that he was laughing at her?

'You must learn not to be a busybody, Miss Darling,' he warned her, and turned to Andrew, but now
his face was relaxed and smiling. 'There are degrees
of poverty,' he stated cheerfully, 'and yes, I suppose
you might say that I am poor in everything that matters most. If I had been in your father's place I daresay I should have said exactly the same thing!'

Andrew nodded, not in the least abashed. 'I
thought you would have. Aunt Cassandra's sorry for
you, aren't you, Aunt Cassandra?' He added in the
tiresome way of small children, 'Why are you frowning, Aunt Cassandra? Are you cross?'

'No!' said his aunt explosively. 'I'm going to help
Jan with the washing up.' She swept out of the room,
considerably hampered by the dressing-gown.

Jan joined her in the kitchen and to her relief

didn't suggest that she returned to the others. They
washed up together and Jan carried on a rather
sketchy conversation to which she paid little attention. She was looking around her as she dried the
bowls and mugs, and she was astonished at what she
saw. The old-fashioned dresser was neatly stacked
with a variety of tinned food of a most expensive
kind; on the kitchen table stood a large wooden box,
its Fortnum and Mason label clearly to be seen; she
glimpsed a half unwrapped York ham inside, and a
Dundee cake wedged beside it. Already on the table,
half unpacked, were a Fuller's chocolate cake, several tins of coq-au-vin, some Stilton cheese and a pot
of Gentleman's Relish. She looked dumbly at Jan,
who took no notice of the look at all, but thanked
her nicely for her help and swept her back into the
sitting-room.

Half an hour later, enveloped in a borrowed
sweater and weighed down by a sheepskin jacket, she
went down the path with Jan, leaving the children,
who didn't seem to mind her going in the least, in
the care of their host while she went to fetch them
some dry clothes.

Once home, she bade Jan make himself comfortable and ran upstairs and pulled on a sweater and
slacks, folded the ogre's sweater neatly, rammed it
and clothes for the children into a hold-all and ran
downstairs again. Five minutes later Jan was on his
way back again.

Later, when he returned with the excited children,

he told her that he would fetch her anorak and bring it to her the next day and she was shocked into exclaiming: 'Indeed no, Jan. I'm perfectly able to fetch it myself.'

'I enjoy the walk, miss,' was what he said, and his tone was final.

She thought about it that night after they were all in bed and the house was quiet. He was such a nice man and though middle-aged, very wiry. True, he was a man of few words, but perhaps his life had made him so. She liked him and the children liked him too, just as they liked the ogre; she had been forced for the rest of the day to listen to their eulogies of him. She was, she told herself, heartily sick of Mr van Manfeld. She was very sorry that he was almost blind, but that was no reason for his deceit; allowing her to make cakes and pies and accepting them as though he had seen nothing better than bread and cheese for weeks. She recalled the well-stocked kitchen and the hamper of delicacies besides. He wasn't poor at all; she would tell him what she thought of him when she saw him again. 'And I hope I don't,' she said aloud, knowing as she said it that she didn't believe her own words.

who told her that he would fetch her anorak and bring it to ask the next day; and she was considerably encouraged by this, and by him. I'm perfectly able to fetch it myself.

So saying, she poured herself out more cold tea and sat

CHAPTER THREE

JAN arrived with the anorak the next morning just as Cassandra and Mrs MacGill were sitting down to a cup of coffee in the bright warm kitchen. The weather had changed overnight; it was overcast, the wind was cold and he looked a little pinched, but when she invited him in to join them, he shook his head and refused in an austere manner.

'Oh, do,' she said coaxingly, and was repelled by the look he gave her. She had thought that what with the home-made cakes, the children's visits and their frightening little adventure, there would have been the beginnings of a real friendship between them, yet now here was Jan demonstrating only too plainly that both he and Mr van Manfeld could do very nicely without her, for of course Mr van Manfeld was at the back of Jan's reluctance. Probably they found her a great nuisance, the children as well. Indeed, casting her mind back, she was able to recall only too clearly the reception she had had on her first visit. She should have learnt a lesson from that; it was her own silly fault. To her intense shame she felt tears prick her eyelids and spill down her cheeks. Without speaking again, Jan turned and walked away down the path, leaving her to shut the door and go upstairs with the anorak, then to the bathroom to wash away the tear marks.

She went down to the village presently and made her modest purchases at the shop, then went back home. The weather hadn't improved, she mooned around the house doing odd jobs which could have waited, then settled down on her hands and knees in the sitting-room, to cut out a dress for Penny. She had brought the material with her from London and Rachel had the last word in sewing machines; she might as well make use of it. She had just started to cut out the fine wool when the doorbell rang and she got to her feet, grumbling a little to herself because she hated to be interrupted when she was cutting out. She opened the door, the scissors in one hand, the tape measure dangling round her neck, and found Mr van Manfeld outside. He gave her no time to speak.

'You cried,' he began at once. 'Jan told me you cried. Why? I really have to know.'

Cassandra opened her mouth, then closed it again, for she could think of nothing to say. When she remained silent, he asked: 'May I come in? I daresay I'm unwelcome, but I've sent Jan on to the village and if you shut the door on me, I shall probably go the wrong way and fall in a ditch—think what shocking headlines that would make! ''Cruel beauty abandons blind man to his fate''—or...'

'Come in, do,' said Cassandra crossly even while she sternly suppressed laughter. 'And how many times do I have to tell you that I'm no beauty?'

He had walked to the centre of the hall. 'Ah, yes,' he said softly, 'I keep forgetting, don't I? A slip of the tongue, shall we say—or an oversensitive imagination.' He turned his face towards her and she saw that he was laughing silently. 'May we stay for tea?' he asked with a meekness which mocked her.

She didn't answer that, but 'Why have you come?' she demanded. 'Jan wouldn't put his foot over the threshold this morning, and I daresay you told him not to.'

'Indeed I did, my dear Cassandra Darling, though I shan't tell you why. He came home mightily upset because you had wept, and told me that I must come and see you because he wouldn't have you made sad. He is fond of you—once upon a time he had a daughter; if she had lived she would have cooked and kept house, just as you do so admirably. One day, when he knows you better, he will tell you about her, I think. It will do him good to talk about her to someone like you. But we digress—why did you cry?'

'Come by the fire,' she said with dignity, 'and I have no intention of telling you, so don't keep on so.'

He had followed her into the sitting-room, feeling around him with his stick as he went. Cassandra pushed a chair out of his way and warned him:

'Keep a little to your left, I'm cutting out a dress for Penny, it's all over the centre of the room.'

When he had settled in the armchair by the fire he continued, just as though he had never paused.

'Much water wears away a stone, and you are no stone, and I am very persistent.'

She put the scissors down on top of the pattern and perched herself on the arm of the chair opposite him. 'I don't intend...' she began.

'Jan and I have been too long by ourselves,' he stated. 'We no longer know how to receive kindness with gratitude, rather we take refuge in bad temper and pride ourselves upon our independence.'

She spoke her thought aloud. 'You told a lie to the children; you said that you were poor.'

'Not quite a lie. I said there were degrees of poverty, did I not? and in the more important aspects of life I am poor. Don't meddle with the context, dear girl, you will become confused. I spoke the truth; I am poor—in friends and affection and laughter and love.'

She went and stood in front of him. Her words tumbled out, one on top of the other. 'It was so unkind—letting me make cakes! I thought you needed—I felt such a fool.'

'That wasn't why you cried.' He got to his feet and put out a hand and touched her uncertainly on her arm. She found herself telling him against her will, 'No, I wanted to be friends, even though you were quite beastly and—and you threw it back at me.' She drew a steadying breath. 'The first time I saw Ogre's Relish I thought how lonely it looked and when the children told me about you—you couldn't see, I wanted—it wasn't curiosity, though I suppose it seemed like that to you.'

'Perhaps, but only for a very short time. You see, you were—are—so refreshingly matter-of-fact about everything. Even in the loch—can you swim, by the way?'

'Well, yes—not very well.'

He laughed and his hand tightened on her arm, then slackened as the door bell rang. 'Jan,' said Cassandra, feeling disappointed although she wasn't sure why. 'I'll let him in.'

It wasn't Jan, it was John Campbell, suitably wrapped against the wind and the soft fine rain which had been falling steadily. He smiled at her and said with ponderous playfulness. 'Good afternoon, Miss Darling. I should be failing in my duties if I didn't call to inquire what kept you from church yesterday. No illness, I trust?'

She had to ask him in. As they crossed the hall she explained in a few words and added, 'Mr van Manfeld is here now, do come and join us.'

Mr Campbell stopped half way across the sitting-room floor. 'I had no idea that you had a visitor,' he protested. 'I'll come some other time, no doubt you wish to be alone…'

'Why?' asked Mr van Manfeld with interest, his face bland. 'I came to see how Cassandra did after her ducking yesterday.'

Mr Campbell was prevailed upon to take a seat and turned his attention upon his fellow caller. 'A pleasure to see you, Mr van Manfeld—we so seldom have an opportunity…' he paused delicately. 'I hope that no damage was done yesterday? Your eyes are in no way affected?'

So he knew all about it already—naturally, in a village as small as this. Cassandra shot a glance towards her other guest, who looked too good to be true with his bland face, only the dark glasses sparkling with hidden mirth; she hoped he would behave himself. She got to her feet and said brightly, 'You'll have a cup of tea? I was just about to put on the kettle.'

The pastor cast a doubtful glance at the ogre, who leaned back a little further in his chair and crossed his legs.

'Do stay, Mr Campbell,' he begged silkily, 'then Cassandra will have to invite me too.'

On her way to the door, she turned sharply, and whatever it was explosive she was about to utter she bit back under Mr Campbell's watchful eye. She addressed the dark glasses in her sweetest tones. 'Oh, I took it for granted that you would stay, Mr van Manfeld. Surely you know me well enough to be certain that I would never send you out into the rain and wind to fall into a ditch?'

This speech was greeted by a bellow of laughter and, from the pastor, a look of pained surprise. Perhaps his sister had been right after all and Miss Darling was indeed one of these heartless modern girls with no pity for others less fortunate than themselves.

'You're old friends,' he inquired cautiously, so that he could account for the laughter.

Mr van Manfeld thought deeply. 'Not really,' he said at length. 'I'm thirty-five—I don't know how old Cassandra is!' He raised his voice to a roar and asked her and she shouted back from the kitchen: 'Twenty-three, why?'

Mr Campbell looked at his companion through narrowed eyes. 'That isn't quite what I meant—no doubt, being a foreigner... Your English is excellent.'

'Cambridge,' said Mr van Manfeld briefly. 'Do you think the weather has broken?'

When Cassandra came back into the room the two men were deep in various aspects of the weather. Mr van Manfeld appeared to be on his best behaviour and she sighed with relief.

They had scones for tea. She poured out, begged the pastor to help himself and explained that she would butter and jam a scone for her other guest.

'One?' his voice was positively plaintive.

She started on a second. 'Two, then, and make them last.' She put the plate on the small table she had set by his chair and guided his hand to it. 'There's the bell, that's Jan. Good, he can have tea too.'

If Jan was surprised to see Mr Campbell he gave no sign, merely wished him a good day, put his packages on the table and sat down and addressed himself to his tea. Cassandra, pouring tea and passing scones, thought that three more ill-assorted guests it would be hard to find; it only needed the children to come in and say something awkward. The wish is father to the thought; it seemed in her case that fears were too; the children did come in, let out of school early for some reason or other. They wished everyone a good afternoon with a politeness which thinly disguised excitement and sat down at their aunt's bidding to their tea. It was the ogre who sat the ball rolling.

'Big with news,' he pronounced. 'I can feel it.' He turned his handsome head in Mr Campbell's direction and explained chattily, 'A lack of sight makes one curiously perceptive to atmosphere. You should try it some time.'

The pastor looked taken aback; to forestall the sermon she could see trembling upon his lips, Cassandra said unwisely, 'News? is there any news, my dears?'

They had been waiting for just such an opening. They spoke together and with a clarity no one could avoid hearing. 'Maggie McLeod's mum says Mr van Manfeld fancies you, Aunt Cassandra,' and as though that wasn't bad enough, 'And Willy MacGregor's dad says you spent the day at Ogre's Relish, and…'

Out of the corner of her eye, Cassandra could see the dark glasses dancing with unholy merriment. She ignored the first remark. 'Of course I was at Ogre's Relish yesterday—so were you—and where else should we have gone but to the nearest house after spending ten minutes in some of the coldest water

I've ever been in?' She glanced at the pastor. 'It's a wonder that Penny and I, let alone Mr van Manfeld, aren't in bed with colds or worse.'

Mr van Manfeld remained silent, contenting himself with looking smugly acquiescent and as if to underline this, took out an enormous and spotless white handkerchief and blew his commanding nose.

Mr Campbell waited until the noise had subsided before he spoke.

'I'm sure there was no other course open to you, Miss Darling. We must all be thankful that rescue was so close at hand. The water is indeed cold in Bru loch, possibly because it is reputed to be bottomless.'

Cassandra choked over her tea. 'Then it was true! How lucky I didn't panic. I should have sunk without trace, and how fortunate that Mr van Manfeld knew how to get us out—we should never have found the place on our own.'

Everyone looked at the ogre and the dark glasses beamed back at them in what Cassandra could only describe to herself as sickening modesty.

She asked, 'Who'd like more tea? And there are heaps more scones in the kitchen. I'll get some fresh tea and another plateful...'

'Allow me,' said Mr Campbell gallantly, and took the teapot from her as the children started off with the empty plate. They all went out of the door together and Jan got up at the same time and went to look out of the window. Cassandra nipped smartly to her feet, went across to Mr van Manfeld's chair and put her face close to his, hissing. 'You're to behave yourself!' and before she could withdraw it he had turned his head and kissed her on the corner of her mouth. There was no time to say all the things which bubbled on her tongue; Mr Campbell was on his way back, she could hear his measured tread in the hall. She cast a look at Jan's back and retreated to her chair just as the foraging party returned.

'So peaceful,' declared Mr Campbell as he entered the room. 'Is there anything better than tea round the fire on a dark afternoon?'

He addressed the room at large and for one awful moment Cassandra was afraid that Mr van Manfeld was going to dispute this opinion, for a wicked little smile hovered round his mouth. Doubtless he was going to make some outrageous remark. She burst into speech herself and saw to her annoyance that the smile had widened.

'Oh, I quite agree,' she said in the unnaturally high voice of a hostess at bay, 'such a pleasant part of the day, but I'm sure the winter is long and dark here, Mr Campbell?'

She sighed with relief as the pastor embarked on a rambling account of winters he had experienced while living on the island, and what with asides about isobars and digressions concerning deep depressions, it took them through the demolition of the scones and the emptying of the teapot and shortly after-wards, as neither of his companions showed signs of going, Mr Campbell rose to his feet. 'I'm glad,' he told Cassandra ponderously, 'that you have taken no harm from your little adventure yesterday. My sister will be delighted to hear of your lucky escape.'

'I thought she already knew,' remarked Cassandra forthrightly, so that he added quickly: 'Oh, yes, but there were various tales—rumours. You know how it is in a small place where everyone knows everyone else.'

'Rumours which I can rely upon you to—er—correct, Mr Campbell?' Mr van Manfeld's voice was soft and he was smiling. Cassandra would have given much to have seen his eyes.

The pastor looked at him a little uncertainly and assured him that he would. As she accompanied him to the door he said in a voice for her ears alone: 'You don't mind? That is, Miss Darling, you have no objection to being left alone with Mr van Manfeld and his servant?'

'They are our friends,' she corrected him gently. 'The children love them dearly and we owe them a great deal, surely you agree with that? Rachel and Tom would wish me to offer them hospitality at the very least.'

He shook her hand. 'Yes, yes, I daresay you're right. I only wish I were in a position to offer you my protection...'

Cassandra withdrew her hand. 'From what?' she asked, 'or should I say from whom? I never felt safer, I assure you, Mr Campbell. It was kind of you to call.' She smiled at him kindly because he was so completely under his sister's thumb. Even now he looked as though he would give anything in the world to recall what he had just said. Taking pity on him, she went on: 'It's very nice to know that you and your sister keep kindly eyes upon us while Tom and Rachel are away.'

The relief on his face rewarded her.

Back in the sitting-room she found Jan organizing the children into a clearing up party and despite her protests, he swept the tea things and the children into the kitchen and within minutes she heard peals of laughter and the sound of him singing.

'That's right, leave him—the children do him good, he's missed so much of life.' The ogre's voice was quiet and she answered him in the same quiet way.

'Yes, I guessed that. He's the nicest man. How old is he?'

'Sixty-three or four, it's not certain.' His voice dared her to ask any more questions and in answer to his unspoken words she said defiantly, 'I shall ask him about his life one day.'

Mr van Manfeld nodded affably. 'Do. What did the reverend gentleman have to say to you in the hall? Don't tell me he was making you a proposal?'

Cassandra rose to the bait. 'And what if he did? Is it so funny that you have to mock him—and me? You behaved very badly.' She stopped, remembering his kiss.

'Did you accept?'

She wasn't a devious girl; she said instantly: 'Of course not, how can you be so foolish?' A thought struck her. 'Or do you think that I should snatch at such a chance—husbands lie rather thin on the ground for plain girls.'

'No, I didn't think that. How you do harp on your lack of looks! I wonder if they're as bad as you make out?'

She got on to her knees and began spreading out the paper pattern again.

'Well,' she snapped her scissors defiantly, 'it doesn't really matter, does it?'

'Meaning that I shall never see you?'

'You said yourself that you were going back soon, and I shall be leaving when Rachel and Tom get back—three weeks.'

'Ah, yes. You wish to further your career. Have you invited us to supper?'

She held the scissors poised and stared at him in astonishment. 'We've only just had tea! The children have their homework to do—at least Andrew has a few sums. We have dripping toast and cocoa round the fire; they go to bed at seven sharp.' She arranged a piece of the pattern carefully. 'Besides, it will be dreadfully dark by then.'

'Jan always carries a torch and the dark doesn't matter to me.'

She said with swift contrition, 'Oh, I'm so sorry! I say such dreadful things—I don't think.'

'I wish everyone behaved as you do, as though I were right in the head and a perfectly normal man. You would be surprised at the number of people who either whisper or shout at me as though I had lost my hearing as well. Supper?'

She laughed. 'Yes, of course, but don't expect anything grand, because you won't get it.'

He smiled. 'That's what I like about you, Cassandra, your warm-hearted hospitality. I'll snap up your generous invitation before we fall out and you show me the door.'

Supper was merry and because the children had to go to bed, quickly over. Andrew, bidden to say goodnight, kissed his aunt and shook hands with the gentlemen, but Penny flung her small arms round Jan's neck and kissed him soundly. She did the same for Mr van Manfeld too, taking much longer about it, and Cassandra, watching with pleased surprise, thought:

'Why, he likes children—really likes them!' For some reason this made her feel very happy.

The two men had their coats on when she came downstairs from tucking the children into their beds. They wished her a cordial good-night, protested that they had had one of the best evenings of their lives, and went out into the pitch darkness, Jan with his torch, his master's hand resting lightly on his other arm. She hoped they would manage; the path was narrow and steep in places and Mr van Manfeld was so very large.

It was a couple of mornings later, in the village shop where she had gone after taking the children to school, that she met Miss Campbell. The place was tolerably full, for no one hurried over their purchases. The pastor's sister made her way between the bags of oatmeal, dog biscuits and mounds of tinned peaches and apricots, treading on indignant toes as she pushed past, and came to a halt before Cassandra, who wished her a polite good morning, remarked upon the weather, which was awful, and consulted her shopping list. But these innocent red herrings did nothing to deter Miss Campbell, who broke into speech without preamble.

'I hear you have been seeing a lot of that peculiar Dutchman who lives like a hermit in the hill croft.'

Cassandra, who seldom blushed, did so now. 'You mean Mr van Manfeld. And it's a cottage, not a croft.'

'Ah, yes, you would know, of course, you have been there.' Miss Campbell tossed her head and her severe felt hat wobbled alarmingly. 'It's all one,' she spoke loudly so that everyone around them could hear. 'And this blindness of his—is it genuine or is it an imagined thing, to draw attention to himself? I cannot think why he hides away when he could be doing useful work of some kind.'

In the silence which followed Cassandra distinctly heard the breathing of the village ladies, waiting to hear what she would say. When she looked around her she found their eyes, to a woman, were friendly.

They gave her heart, so that when she did speak her voice was clear and calm with no trace of the rage which was almost choking her.

'I'm surprised at your question, Miss Campbell,' she began. 'It's uncharitable, and isn't charity a Christian virtue, one surely which you, as the pastor's sister, must possess? I hesitate to discuss Mr van Manfeld behind his back, but I must correct you on one or two points. He *is* blind, or nearly so. Can you imagine a world where everything is dark blue and nothing has shape or form, only movement? And yet he jumped into the loch to get Penny and me out, you know. The pastor must have told you that, for he had tea with us all the other afternoon. Surely ploughing through ice-cold water when you can't see is more of a Christian act than going to church and criticizing your neighbour's hat? And what would you do if you were suddenly to lose your sight and knew that your chances of regaining it depended upon living as quiet a life as possible? And would you want to be stared at and pitied? And what work would *you* do in those circumstances?'

She stopped, breathing heavily, holding back rage, aware that in Miss Campbell she had an enemy for life while at the same time everyone else in the shop was on her side. She smiled round a little uncertainly, wished Miss Campbell a cold good-day and made for the door. Jan was standing just inside it; he must have heard every word, the look on his face confirmed this. He would go back and tell Mr van Man-

feld what she had said and he would come storming
down to rend her with his rage and bad language for
daring to interfere in his affairs.

She returned home, expecting, at any hour, a sharp
ring on the door bell heralding an irate Mr van Manfeld, but no one came—no one came the next day
either. It was the day following that when Jan appeared silently beside her in the cold garden where
she was sweeping up the dead leaves. It was early
afternoon; the children were back at school and the
short hours before teatime had to be filled, the evening would be long enough after the children were
in bed and she was alone with the TV, her embroidery and her not very happy thoughts.

He wished her a good afternoon and asked her if
she would go back with him to the Relish.

'Why?' she wanted to know, leaning on her besom.

'Mijnheer would like to see you.'

'I'm rather busy,' she began, fighting a strong desire to throw down the broom and tear up the path
without waiting for Jan. She didn't stop to analyse
this wish. 'Another day perhaps.'

Jan eyed her thoughtfully. 'Sometimes Mijnheer
has severe head pains.' He tapped his own balding
head to emphasize his meaning. 'The swim in the
loch did him no good. He is better today.'

Now she threw down the besom. 'Oh, Jan, why
didn't you let me know sooner? Perhaps there was
something I could have done. I'll come right away.'

She glanced at her watch. 'The children won't be out of school for almost two hours.'

She dragged on the anorak, snatched up the house keys and joined him in the garden, then saw him glance at her empty hands. 'He's got plenty of cakes,' she said defensively. 'I saw them…'

'Not yours, miss. He likes them.'

Cassandra went back into the house. She had had a baking day; she wrapped up a cherry cake, and put it into a basket and rejoined Jan. They were at the cottage in no time at all; Jan was a good walker despite his age and she had long legs which made light of the climb. Jan opened the door and Mr van Manfeld turned his head towards them from his chair by the fire. 'There you are!' he declared. 'And about time—what have you been doing? Half the afternoon is gone.'

'Don't exaggerate,' said Cassandra. 'It's not quite half past two and we simply tore up the path.' She cast off her anorak and went to stand by his chair. 'I'm sorry to hear you haven't been well—I feel so guilty, because I'm sure that you should never have gone in after Penny and me.'

'Oh, be quiet,' he snapped. 'It couldn't be helped, if it hadn't been me it would have been some other fool.' He frowned fiercely, not troubling to turn his head towards her. She sighed soundlessly. It was to be a bad-tempered day; she wondered how Jan kept his cool as she knelt down beside the chair and said reasonably, 'You feel rotten, don't you? Do spew your venom over me, you'll feel so much better for it—you're worried that some damage has been done, aren't you? It's all bottled up, you know, and that doesn't do you any good at all.'

His hand felt for and found her shoulder. 'Sound advice—what a girl you are! I've driven poor Jan almost insane these last two days, I don't know how he bears with me.'

'You bore with me, *mijnheer*, and I don't forget.' Jan's voice was quiet. 'I will make a cup of tea, I think.' He went into the kitchen.

'What does he mean?' asked Cassandra.

Mr van Manfeld frowned horribly. 'Nothing—nothing at all.'

Something for later, she promised herself; she would find out. She said boldly, 'Tell me about your work, Mr van Manfeld.'

He scowled. 'Ear, nose and throat. I've a partner.'

'Consultant?'

'Yes.'

'And beds in hospital somewhere?' she persisted.

'Yes.' After a moment he added reluctantly, 'Arnhem, Nijmegen—most in Utrecht.'

'Not just Ts and As, then?'

He smiled faintly. 'I'm interested in CA of the larynx and vocal cords.'

'With success?'

'Sometimes. I was just getting somewhere…'

'And will again,' she said briskly. 'You're keeping

up to date? Does Jan read the medical journals to you?'

Before Mr van Manfeld could reply Jan answered for him. 'I try, miss, but the medical terms I find rather difficult. There is a journal come today.' He put down the tea tray and went to fetch it—*World Medicine*, not even opened. She glanced at Jan, who nodded his head, and started to unwrap the cake.

'Would you like me to read it to you?' she asked, and had her head snapped off with: 'That's quite unnecessary! You'll be bringing me hot soup and a prayer next!'

She laid the journal down on the table beside him and got to her feet. 'I don't think I'll stay for tea,' she declared cheerfully. 'I'm wasting your time, and I'm certainly wasting mine.' She whisked up her anorak and started to put it on. She actually had one arm in a sleeve when he said crossly, 'I should very much like you to read to me.'

'In that case I'll stay.'

Cassandra read, in her quiet, pretty voice, for an hour, re-reading bits here and there and getting up to hunt through the piles of books lying around the room to check some reference or other. She had to go in the end because the children had to be fetched from school. As she got ready to leave she remarked, 'I enjoyed that. I've never worked in ENT theatre, although learning about it isn't quite the same as seeing it done.'

Mr van Manfeld was sitting back, smoking his

pipe. 'No—you would find the theatre work interesting, I believe. So many people dismiss it as tonsils and adenoids.'

She laughed with him. 'Perhaps I'll get around to it later on.'

'Perhaps. Cassandra, thank you for this afternoon. I do not know how you are able to turn my nightmares to day-dreams, but you do. Will you come again?'

'Tomorrow, to read to you. Silly of me not to have thought of it sooner.' She paused. 'That's if Jan doesn't mind?'

'Jan is delighted, aren't you, Jan?'

The older man nodded, his dark sombre face split in a wide smile. 'You like me to come with you, miss?' he asked her.

'No, thanks, Jan. I'll be up about the same time tomorrow.'

She went every afternoon after that, reading to a surprisingly meek ogre, listening intelligently to his theories—and he had many—searching carefully for notes and references he wanted read again. It was only on the fourth afternoon, just as she was on the point of leaving, that he said, 'Just a minute, Cassandra. Thank you for defending me so well—Jan told me. Miss Campbell is a formidable opponent, I gather.'

'I thought you'd be angry, but I had to put her right—heaven knows what tale she would have spread around the village. Only I didn't tell her what you are.'

'So I gather. Thank you for being so thoughtful. They'll forget me once we've left.'

She was shaken by a dreadful sadness. 'Oh? When's that?'

'Soon, I hope. It's Saturday tomorrow. Will you bring the children and we might all go for a walk.'

Cassandra went back home, telling herself that she would forget him too once he had gone and quite failing to convince herself on this point. And the children certainly wouldn't—they were wild with delight when she passed on his invitation.

It was the middle of the following week when Jan came down one morning and asked her not to go that afternoon. He gave no explanation and she asked for none, but she thought about it quite a bit while she did the ironing. A visitor, perhaps? She was surprised to think that she had never given consideration to the fact that Mr van Manfeld might be married; if so she didn't think much of his wife, leaving him to solitude with only Jan for company, but perhaps there were small children. Was that why he was so fond of Penny and Andrew? She found it strangely disquieting; perhaps even at that moment his wife—or his girl-friend for that matter—was sitting up there with him and he was telling them about the plain-faced girl who had infringed upon his privacy, or perhaps he didn't even bother to mention her? She banged the iron down too hard and made a crease where there shouldn't have been one, so that she had to start all over again.

She didn't go the next afternoon either; better to wait until he sent a message. He didn't; he came himself the following morning very early. Cassandra had returned from taking the children to school and was in the kitchen polishing Rachel's table silver when she heard Mrs Todd go to the door, and being Mrs Todd, she didn't show him into the sitting-room but led him across the back of the hall and into the kitchen.

'Good heavens!' exclaimed Cassandra, and felt happy surprise at the sight of him. 'Whatever brings you here? Is Jan ill? Come into the sitting-room...'

'Not even a good morning,' complained Mr van Manfeld. 'In your anxiety to hear about Jan, who is perfectly well—what are you doing?'

'Cleaning the silver.'

'In that case I will stay here with you, if I may. I wish to talk to you.'

She glanced at his face and wished for the hundredth time that she could see his eyes. His face told her nothing, but he wouldn't walk down at this hour of the day for no reason at all. 'Where's Jan?' she asked.

'Gone to the village. I had a visitor.'

'I thought perhaps you had.'

'I'm going back to Holland for some further tests—it seems there has been unexpected progress.'

She picked up the coffee spoons and put them

down again. 'Oh, your doctor!' and felt a surge of relief.

'Who else?' asked Mr van Manfeld sharply, then laughed. 'Romantic as well as a busybody,' he added silkily.

'You have no need to be rude,' she reminded him. 'You know I take no notice.'

'I know, that's why I'm here. I want you to come back to Holland with me.' He grinned suddenly. 'As my nurse, of course.'

Cassandra picked up the spoons again, looked at them as though she had never seen them before and stacked them neatly. 'I'm afraid I can't accept your offer. You see...'

'Not very well,' he interposed dryly, and the vexed colour ran into her face.

'You have a horrid way of putting me at a disadvantage!' she snapped.

'My apologies,' his voice was bland, never had it sounded so unapologetic. 'You have applied for your midder training?'

She hadn't. At a disadvantage, she flared: 'I'm— I—it's no concern of yours what I do!'

The dark glasses were turned on her, it was like being held in the glare of a searchlight. 'I thought,' he commented softly, 'that I had the monopoly of rudeness.'

'I'm sorry. The trouble is we're both so independent, aren't we? You see, I can think of no reason why you should want a nurse—me—to go back to Holland with you.'

The grim look on his face dissolved. 'In that case, have the goodness to hear me out before you start putting difficulties in the way. I need a nurse—oh, not to wash my face and lead me around, but someone who will stand between me and my impatience—my rage, if you prefer, someone to get between me and the pity I am bound to encounter, someone to remind me to use my eye-drops on time and stop me taking my glasses off, someone to listen when I blow my top, someone who has no axe to grind and no fondness for me so that she doesn't feel the need to hedge me in from everyday things. A soft-hearted dragon, Cassandra—and you fill the bill very nicely.' He added, suddenly irritable, 'I can't be as bad as all that, and it will only be for a couple of weeks, perhaps less.'

'What happens then?' she wanted to know. 'You go into the operating theatre without glasses, I suppose, and then wonder why you have a headache and can't see a thing!'

He laughed so that he looked much younger and the idea of calling him Mr van Manfeld seemed all of a sudden absurd. But she didn't know his name.

'Sensible Cassandra! It is to be hoped that in that time you will have forced me into so strict a routine that I shan't dare to change it. Let us be serious. If everything goes well, I may be allowed to use my eyes—tinted glasses, of course—and start work, consulting and the practice. The theatre will have to wait.'

Cassandra stopped fidgeting with the silver and walked round the table. 'It's wonderful news,' she told him. 'I should have said that first, shouldn't I? I'm very happy for you—you'll go back to Holland and forget all this.'

'No, I'll not forget,' he spoke quietly, his face turned away. 'You won't come. I'm sorry.' He got to his feet. 'It's a pleasant morning even though it's cold,' he informed her conversationally. 'I think I'll go and meet Jan; I know the track well enough.'

If he had sworn at her or displayed his icy ill-humour or even sneered just once, she would have held out against him, even though she longed to go with him. It was ridiculous that a giant of a man could manage to look so lost and pathetic. She got to the door just ahead of him.

'No—that is, yes, I'll come. Just for a week or two, but it's crazy! I can't speak Dutch and I'll lose my place for my midwifery training—and anyway I can't go until Rachel comes back.'

He loomed over her; he didn't look lost or pathetic at all, and although his face was carefully smooth the glasses gave the game away; they were dazzling in their triumph.

'Why,' she began, 'you…'

'You promised, Cassandra, just this minute. God's teeth, for one awful moment I thought you wouldn't come…'

'I wish you wouldn't say that,' she said waspishly. 'And now see what you've made me do!'

He caught her hand. 'Dear girl, you have only to say that you won't come and we'll forget the whole thing. I admit I acted a little deceptively.' He sighed and took her other hand. 'I want to get back to work,' his voice was serious now, 'and I think you're the one person who can help me.'

Put like that, she could see reason for his persistence. 'Very well, but I've just told you, I can't go until Rachel…'

'Gets back. Let me see, that will be on December the second, if Penny had her dates right. We'll leave the day after that.'

'I've no uniform,' she said weakly. 'I couldn't possibly.'

'Buy it—surely in Oban you can get something? You're a tall girl, from the sound of your voice—are you big with it? Do you have to have things made to measure?'

Cassandra choked. 'You're abominable!' she managed. 'I'm quite tall, but I'm not—not outsize.'

He grinned. 'I'll not comment. Buy what you need and send the bills to me.'

'Certainly not!'

'Cassandra, you will do as I ask. What salary were you receiving at the hospital?' She told him. 'A pittance,' he snorted, and named a sum well in excess of it. 'And don't dare to argue,' he finished in a voice which brooked none.

'Very well,' she found herself answering him

meekly, 'but you're paying me much too much, you know.'

He was still holding her two hands. 'I tell you, Cassandra, if the tests aren't successful, you will deserve every penny of your salary.'

She agreed with him silently; the possibility didn't bear thinking of, the thought of him never seeing again hurt her. She said sturdily:

'You're not to talk like that—they're going to be one hundred per cent successful.'

He smiled. 'You have a passport?'

'Yes. How shall we go?'

'By plane to Schipol—drive from there. There'll be a day or two at home before I have the tests.' He gave her back her hands and bent to kiss her gently. 'There's Jan at the door.'

Jan was admitted and told the news, and she saw the satisfaction on his dark face. He nodded to himself, smiled at her and said, 'This is a good thing, miss! You wish to keep it a secret, *mijnheer*?' he spoke to Mr van Manfeld.

'No,' drawled the ogre, 'if we keep it a secret it's sure to leak out, and that would hardly do. We'll tell everyone, including the children.' He felt around for his stick. 'Jan, we must go. Cassandra, you will come and read to me this afternoon?'

It sounded like a command, but nicely put. She said that she would.

The children, though crestfallen at the idea of losing their ogre, were excited to hear that their aunt would be going to Holland with him.

'To marry him, Aunt Cassandra, and live happy ever after?' asked Penny.

Cassandra stared at her niece. How wonderful it would be if she could say yes to that question! She dismissed the foolish idea and answered in a practical voice. 'No, love. As his nurse. He needs someone to help him for a little while. Jan will have enough to do without looking after Mr van Manfeld as well.'

'Perhaps when you've finished being his nurse,' persisted Penny, to be interrupted by Andrew, who said loudly, 'Don't be a silly little girl! The ogre will marry a princess with golden hair like those stupid fairy stories Aunt Cassandra reads you.'

His aunt cast him a smouldering look. What chance had she if a six-year-old dismissed her so swiftly from the matrimonial scene? And hadn't Mr van Manfeld called her a dragon? With a heart of gold, it was true, but what was the use of that? No one could see it, only the dragon's exterior. She sighed to herself and went to fetch her raincoat, for the rain was coming down in earnest now.

She was a little prim that afternoon, reading non-stop and very correctly, glad for once that her companion couldn't see her. When she got up to go he asked her, 'Overwhelmed, Cassandra, or regretting your promise?' And when she didn't answer, went on, 'I don't have to see to know that something's worrying you.'

She denied it vigorously. How to tell him that she was bowed down with the knowledge that he thought of her as a dragon?

CHAPTER FOUR

WITHIN hours the village knew. Cassandra, who preferred to take the bull by the horns rather than wait
to be gored by it, went into Mrs MacGill's shop that
afternoon for some quite unnecessary sugar, and was
greeted by that lady's 'Weel, so ye're off to foreign
parts, I hear, Miss Cassandra.'

There were two other ladies in the shop; they
would spread the news around very nicely. 'That's
right, Mrs MacGill,' Cassandra agreed pleasantly.
'Mr van Manfeld is going back to his home for some
tests on his eyes and he'll need a good deal of help—
in and out of hospital and so forth,' she added, em-
broidering it a little. 'The specialist who saw him the
other day hopes that his sight is returning, but it may
mean patience for that.'

'What does he do exactly?' asked Mrs MacGill.

The time seemed ripe to allow the village in on
the ogre's well-kept secret. 'He's an ear, nose and
throat specialist, he did a great deal of operating and
hopes to do so again.'

'A doctor!' breathed Mrs MacGill erroneously.
'Now that's an entirely different kettle of fish, the
puir man. Married?' She flung the question at Cas-

87

sandra like a bullet from a gun, but Cassandra was ready for her.

'Wedded to his work,' she assured her audience solemnly, and departed with her bags of sugar, well content with her work.

It all came back to her, of course. That very afternoon as she sat reading an article on Vincent's Angina to Mr van Manfeld, Jan came back with his own shopping. He paused just inside the door and said: '*Mijnheer*, you have become a saint within a few hours—you are a world-famous specialist, so great and good that you have no eyes for women.'

His employer sat up slowly. 'Jan, have you been drinking?'

'No, *mijnheer*, this is what I am told in the shop.'

'Well, they're rather wide of the mark,' conceded the ogre mildly, 'except the bit about having no eyes for the women—just let them wait until I get my eyes back!'

Cassandra had no doubt of that. She said now in a small voice, 'I'm afraid I...'

Her host rounded on her. 'Don't tell me—Miss Busybody again! Now what have you said?'

'Nothing much,' she told him, 'and I only added the bit about you being wedded to your work,' she faltered at the look he gave her, 'because I didn't know.'

'You astonish me—didn't know what?'

'If you're married, or—or...'

'Ah, yes, how very tactful of you, Cassandra. I can

see that you will be of the greatest possible help to me in the next few weeks.'

Such an unsatisfactory answer, she fumed to herself as she went home.

She had the opportunity of telling Rachel all about it that evening when her sister telephoned, and Rachel had been astounded and then a little apprehensive.

'Couldn't he have got a Dutch nurse?' she asked cautiously. 'I mean, did you tell him you were waiting to fill a vacancy for your midwifery? And what will you do about that? They'll never hold it for you.'

Cassandra had had plenty of time to think about that. 'I'll do private nursing for a month or two,' she told her sister, 'and apply for the next course; you see, he needs someone from this end—for the journey and so on, Jan will have enough to do.' Even in her own ears it didn't sound very convincing. She began to wonder herself why Mr van Manfeld hadn't arranged to be met by a nurse in Holland. She would ask him.

She did, a day or so later when she had gone up the hill to read to him.

He had turned the dark glasses upon her and said coolly, 'I should have thought you would have known that without having to ask me. I know you well enough to be sure that you won't run screaming from the house if I happen to lose my temper; that you'll steer me through the tests with the minimum of fuss; that if things go wrong you'll not panic or drip useless tears over me. What had your sister to say about it?'

'Well—she, that is, she was surprised.'

He laughed. 'Horrified too, I suspect, that her young, untried sister is about to embark on a job with a foreigner of whom she knows nothing.'

Cassandra said calmly, 'Something like that. Only we know it's not like that, so that I don't see that it matters what anyone else thinks.'

'The more I see of you—metaphorically speaking, my dear Cassandra Darling—the more I am convinced that I have unearthed a treasure. I should like to meet your sister—I have already met your brother-in-law briefly. Could you arrange that?'

'Yes, of course. Will you come down or will they come up?'

'I'll come down—with Jan, of course.'

Cassandra got up to go. She was pulling on her gloves and making rather a work of it before she spoke again. 'Look, Rachel is sure to ask if there's a housekeeper or—or someone…'

'I should expect that. You had forgotten to ask me that question, had you not? Or is your faith in me so touching that you found it unnecessary?'

'I forgot,' she answered him shortly because there was a mocking little smile on his lips. 'I'm asking now.'

'Set your mind at rest, I have arranged for an aunt—an elderly aunt—to stay with me for a short time. There is also Miep, who cooks and housekeeps for me. Satisfied?'

'Quite.' She heard her voice quiver hatefully. 'You have the most unpleasant way of making me feel a fool, Mr van Manfeld, and as far as I can see, I haven't earned it.'

She bounced through the door and was on the point of shutting it when his voice arrested her. 'Have we quarrelled,' he asked mildly, 'or will you come tomorrow?'

She raced down the path, her ill humour giving her long legs a fine turn of speed. He was the most annoying man! For two pins she would change her mind and not go with him. He would be able to manage quite well without her, for Jan had looked after him all these weeks. Reason reminded her that now that he was to be examined exhaustively, entailing visits to hospital, doctors' consulting rooms and the like, Jan might not have the time to cope. She wasn't sure, but she believed that the older man acted as general factotum in the surgeon's house; once they were back in Holland, he would have enough to do without accompanying him here, there and everywhere. She dismissed the subject from her mind, whistled to Bob and went to fetch the children. It was only a job, after all, and a very temporary one at that.

The remaining days before Rachel and Tom returned flew by. Cassandra and Mrs Todd cleaned the house, polished silver and windows and Cassandra spent almost all of one day in the kitchen, cooking. Even so, she managed to visit Mr van Manfeld most afternoons, and the children seized every opportunity of visiting him too. She had seen nothing more of the pastor or his sister; probably he felt that he should avoid her since she and Miss Campbell had their altercation. She was surprised, therefore, to find him on the doorstep when she answered the doorbell the day before Rachel and Tom were due back. She invited him in, thankful that she wasn't doing anything in particular for an hour or so. He followed her into the sitting-room and sat down and she perched on the chair opposite, saying in her friendly way, 'I'll make tea presently—it's a little early.'

Mr Campbell looked up nervously. 'Oh, no tea, thank you, Miss Cassandra, I can stay only a few minutes, but despite my sister's advice I felt that I must come and see you.'

Cassandra felt a pang of pity for his worried look. 'That's kind of you,' she murmured, and smiled helpfully.

'It is my duty,' he went on, adopting the sonorous tones which she recognized as those he used when he was preparing to embark on his Sunday sermon. 'I hear from various sources that you contemplate returning to Holland with Mr van Manfeld. I can only deplore this decision, my dear young lady. Doubtless you are going in the role of nurse, but I feel strongly that a nurse could be obtained in Holland and I can see no reason for your going.'

Cassandra stifled an urge to speak her mind, but she supposed he meant it kindly. She said reasonably, 'No, I don't expect you do.' After all, the poor man had doubtless been fed a great number of unlikely stories. She went on: 'Mr van Manfeld does need help on the journey, you know. Jan will have the luggage to see to and so on. And in Holland there'll be plenty for me to do—treatment, preparation for the tests, going to the hospital. I think that you—everyone—forgets that I'm a nurse with my living to earn. If I didn't look after Mr van Manfeld I should look after someone else, man, woman or child—all's grist that comes to my mill.' She smiled at him and added gently, 'I shall be in uniform all the time.'

It seemed a silly remark, but she could see that it carried great weight with him for it conjured up a picture of herself, no longer a girl but a nurse, different, aloof, and above the wild temptations Mr Campbell so obviously had in mind.

'That is, of course, different.' He put his hands together and tapped his fingers gently one against the other. 'I wonder if I should have a word with Mr van Manfeld.'

Cassandra eyed him with some alarm. 'I don't think that would be necessary, Mr Campbell. He's a distinguished surgeon in his own country, he has a reputation to maintain; he's unlikely to do anything which would injure that in any way.'

She had said just the right thing again. Mr Campbell relaxed at last and when she suggested tea again, agreed to a hasty cup. Over it he remarked: 'I am sorry that my sister...' He looked at her anxiously. 'She is a little out of this world,' he offered.

And you can say that again! thought Cassandra to herself, and asked after the garden which she knew was his pride and joy.

It was half an hour later, on the doorstep saying goodbye, that Mr Campbell said suddenly: 'Despite your assurances, Miss Cassandra, I think it may be a good idea if I go and have a little talk with the doctor—man to man, you know. I hope you agree?'

'No, I don't,' said Cassandra bluntly, 'and he's not a doctor, he's a surgeon.' She envisaged a lively picture of the ogre involved in a manly talk with her companion and eyed him with pity. She began: 'I'm sure there's no need...'

He took one of her hands and patted it. 'Allow me to be the best judge of that, my dear young lady,' he begged her.

He was barely through the garden gate when she left the house herself with Bob lumbering along beside her. She must fetch the children from school and go straight to Ogre's Relish. They greeted the news that they were to pay their ogre a visit with glee.

At the door, with Cassandra's hand lifted to ply the knocker, it was arrested by the sound of Mr van Manfeld's voice. 'Where the hell have you put them?' he was demanding in a subdued roar which penetrated the stout door without diminishing its strength. The children exchanged delighted glances tinged with delicious fright—their ogre was at last behaving like one—but their aunt only sighed as she applied herself to the knocker. It was one of those days; she needed no second sight to know that.

There was a brief silence before Mr van Manfeld shouted impatiently: 'Well, come in, whoever you are!'

Upon this far from welcoming note, they entered. He was standing in the centre of the room, his head almost to the ceiling, the dark glasses, turned in their direction, sparking off ill-temper.

'Oh, it's you,' he said at once, and added nastily, 'We've had tea.'

'Tea?' echoed Cassandra. 'From the sound of you it wasn't tea, but a nice strong cup of fuming sulphuric acid.'

She watched a reluctant smile tug at the corners of his mouth. 'You didn't come this afternoon—Jan's packing and I've been sitting and thinking.'

'And now your world is darker than ever; the tests have failed, the future is empty, nobody loves you and life is no longer to be borne.' Her voice was brisk and kind. 'You shouldn't allow your imagination to run away with you, Mr van Manfeld.' And because the smile was turning into a scowl, she went on: 'Do you suppose the children could go with Jan for a few minutes? I have to talk to you.'

A questioning look supplanted the scowl, but all he said was, 'Of course', and shouted through the door to Jan, who came silently, nodded and smiled at her and took Andrew and Penny away.

'What a marvellous man,' commented Cassandra, and meant it.

'My lifeline,' said Mr van Manfeld shortly. 'Now, what can I do for you? Sit down, do.'

She sat and waited while he made his way to his own chair and settled into it. 'Mr Campbell came to see me this afternoon—he's only just gone. He's worried about me going to Holland with you. I know it's none of his business, but he thinks—that is, he's coming to see you to have a man-to-man talk.'

The dark glasses gave nothing away. 'Indeed?' queried her companion silkily. 'Should I feel flattered?' He remained silent briefly and then snapped: 'Why?'

'Well,' she began, 'it's like this—that is—it's me going with you—he's old-fashioned, and when I told him that I should be wearing uniform he seemed to think it would be all right.' She was stopped by Mr van Manfeld's shout of laughter, but she ignored it. 'I told him that you were a well-known surgeon and had your reputation to consider...' Her voice faltered and died under the glasses' glare.

'I'll wring his neck!' declared the ogre softly.

'No, you mustn't do that, it would cause so many complications.' She spoke seriously and couldn't think why he smiled suddenly. 'You could be in bed with a headache or having a bath, or...'

He said, his voice still very soft, 'My ingenious,

anxious Cassandra, I shall be sitting here waiting for him; he shall have his man-to-man talk and I promise you that he will go away quite satisfied as to my— er—lack of dishonourable intentions.' He smiled at her and looked just as she had known in her heart he had looked before he had lost his sight: safe and calm and utterly dependable. She sighed without knowing that she did so, and got to her feet.

'I had to tell you,' she explained. 'I feel very mean, it's like telling tales to get someone into trouble, but I thought you might misunderstand—he meant it kindly.'

He put out a hand and she took it. 'Of course you had to tell me. I might have killed the man unless I had received your warning, and don't worry, Cassandra, I shan't cast you in the role of perfidious Albion. I find Campbell's action most offensive, but I'll do nothing, you have my word.'

She collected the children then went back home to tea. Mr van Manfeld might have a shocking bad temper, he might be used to having his own way and having, she suspected, the best of everything, but on one point she was quite certain, he wouldn't break a promise once he had given it. All the same, she found herself wishing that she could be there when the two men had their little talk.

Rachel and Tom arrived home by lunchtime. They had travelled up by the night train from London and with two excited children, who had been excused school for the day, Cassandra drove down to the ferry to pick them up. The six weeks had gone very quickly, she thought, standing back to allow the children to get at their parents. Rachel looked lovely, brown and almost plump—it suited her, and Tom looked as rested as well as happy.

At home again, Rachel asked about the children, their manners, school, Mr Campbell, his sister and whether Mrs Todd had coped with the housework, and only when they had run through these pressing matters did she inquire casually, 'And this Dutchman—the one the children call the ogre—how did you come to meet him in the first place?'

Cassandra thought. 'Well, I went up there—to Ogre's Relish, the children told me about him and he sounded lonely.'

'I see. And was he glad to see you?'

'He can't see,' corrected Cassandra. 'No, he wasn't at all pleased. He ordered me off, but then he came down here and said he was sorry, and the children like him.'

Mr van Manfeld arrived that evening after dinner and was immediately engulfed in the children's fervent embraces. He disentangled himself gently, apologized with charm for the delay this caused in greeting his host and hostess and introduced the silent Jan. Cassandra in the kitchen, putting the final touches to the coffee tray, heard the hubbub and came out into the hall, saying in a matter-of-fact voice, 'Oh, there you are! What a good thing you've come, now perhaps the children will go to bed.'

She smiled at everyone, feeling happy, and urged her nephew and niece towards the stairs and skipped up after them. She was down again quite soon to find the company already in the sitting-room.

It was obvious that Mr van Manfeld was making a good impression upon his host and hostess. Later that evening, when the two men had gone, Rachel, over a last cup of coffee, remarked: 'You were very quiet, darling—I must admit I found your ogre rather a sweetie.'

And Tom, from behind his paper, mumbled, 'Yes, nice chap. No side. I like the fellow— Cassy will be quite safe with him.'

Cassandra smiled and said nothing at all. Mr van Manfeld was a cunning rascal, pretending to be someone he wasn't—at least— She was suddenly uncertain; perhaps he really was like that, perhaps once they were in Holland and with the prospect of his career continuing, even if to a lesser degree, he would become remote, engrossed in his work, polite, never call her Cassandra but address her as nurse and not lose his temper once.

They were to leave by the morning ferry and be driven by hired car to Glasgow airport, a journey of somewhat less than ninety miles, and Tom was to drive Cassandra down to the boat, where she would join Mr van Manfeld and Jan. It was a sparkling morning and cold in the lingering darkness trailed by the winter night.

There was barely time to greet her fellow passen-

gers, wish everyone else good-bye and board the
ferry. It wasn't really light yet; she quickly lost sight
of the little pier and the group of people standing on
it, peering back at the fast receding outline of the
island, she reflected that it scarcely seemed like six
weeks since she had arrived. She wondered what the
next six weeks would hold for her.

Their journey was uneventful and undertaken in
extreme comfort. It seemed no time at all before they
were leaving Schipol's Customs hall and walking towards the air terminal's exit. Just before they reached
it, Mijnheer van Manfeld said, 'We shall wait here
while Jan fetches the car,' and allowed himself to be
guided to a seat. She would dearly have liked to
know how her patient's car had got to the airport,
but she didn't like to ask. He had grown a little silent
during the last hour; she didn't think he was tired,
just thoughtful. Presumably when he wished to talk,
he would do so. She sat quietly beside him and presently he remarked:

'How serene you are, dear girl—no fidgeting with
your hair, no opening and shutting of your handbag,
no sighing—above all, no questions.'

A remark which effectively prevented her from
asking several which were on the tip of her tongue
at that moment.

Jan was only away for a very short time. She saw
him coming towards them and touched the man beside her on the arm. 'Here's Jan. He's stopped to see
about the luggage, but I think he's ready for us.'

They gained the outside of the building without mishap and found Jan, who had gone ahead of them, stowing the luggage away in the car. Despite the early evening dark she was able to see it in the airport's lights—an Aston Martin DBS V8, sleek and rakish, not at all the kind of car she imagined the ogre would have driven, and yet, now she thought about it, probably he was a fast driver in normal circumstances. Mr van Manfeld settled back in his corner with the air of a caged lion selecting the best bars to lean against.

'In answer to your unspoken question,' he remarked as the car slid forward, 'we have a journey of roughly forty-five miles, most of it on a motorway, which you will find very dull, I'm afraid, even in the dark. But at Ochten we shall turn off on to a smaller road. I shall take a nap, be good enough to waken me when we reach the bridge over the Rhine.'

She stole a look at him presently. Presumably he had closed his eyes on his dark blue world. It was impossible to tell; the glasses had dark side pieces and they fitted closely in all directions. For all she knew he might even now be peering sideways at her, a dark blob against a darker background, but he made no movement; the straight, disdainful nose contrived to look disdainful even while he slept; his mouth was firmly closed. Either he was asleep already or he was hiding behind his glasses. She made herself look out of the window, which was stupid anyway, for by now it was quite dark even though the sky was clear and there was an icy moon beaming down on to the motorway. And how was she to identify a bridge when they came to it? She tried to see the time by her watch with no success at all—he had said forty-five miles; at the speed they were going and the fact that there seemed to be no hills and no corners, she judged that they would be at their destination within three-quarters of an hour. Suddenly the moon, coming out from behind a cloud, sparkled on water and in the distance ahead of them she saw a line of lights. She said triumphantly:

'I think we're at the bridge.'

Her companion stirred. 'Jan?'

'Just coming on to it now, *mijnheer*. Miss Cassandra is observant.'

They were crossing the river now, the twinkling lights quite near, the outline of a great church loomed up suddenly and they were off the bridge, going slowly in the narrow streets leading up past the church to the main street of Rhenen. The shops were still open with decorated windows and bright lights. Cassandra sat forward the better to see.

'The shops are so gay,' she told her companion, 'lighted up and full of people. The street is packed!'

'Of course, it is Sint Nicolaas the day after tomorrow. It rivals Christmas in Holland.'

'You're glad you're back home for it.' She stated the fact simply.

'Yes,' but he didn't say any more, not until Jan

turned the car down a narrow street leading back towards the river, and stopped almost immediately.

'Home,' said Mijnheer van Manfeld briefly, and Jan got out to help Cassandra out of the car. She stood on the pavement in the cold evening, looking around her, while Jan went to help his master. The house before which they had stopped was one of a row, all of them several stories high, all with large windows and massive front doors. As she looked at it, the lights snapped on in the downstairs windows and the door was flung open, to reveal a large woman with a massive bosom and a quantity of white hair. She didn't wait for Mr van Manfeld to ascend the three steps leading to his door, but came down them to the pavement, where she shook him by the hand at great length, talking animatedly as she did so. Surely not the elderly aunt, thought Cassandra, and heard her patient say: 'Cassandra, go inside, it's too cold for you to stand about. Jan?'

Jan touched her arm. 'This way, Miss Cassandra. Mijnheer is a little hindered. That is Miep, the cook and housekeeper who has been with him for a great deal of his life—she has a fondness for him.'

She had her foot on the top step when Jan disappeared and it was the ogre beside her, 'Welcome to my home, Cassandra,' he said quietly. 'I hope that you will be happy here.'

She stood, half in, half out, looking up at him, perfectly certain that she was going to be happy. For would she not be with him for most of the days ahead, and wasn't that what she wanted more than anything in the world? She admitted it to herself at last; the ogre wasn't an ogre at all but the man she had fallen in love with. Even as she admitted it she told herself crossly that she was a fool. She had had no success with the Registrar—she tried to remember his name; what he looked like, and couldn't; she needn't expect any success with the man beside her either. Probably he had dozens of girl-friends; he might be engaged; she thought it very likely, and now she came to think about it, he had never said that he wasn't married. She lifted her firm little chin; she wouldn't cross her bridges until she came to them, she would be his dragon because that was what he had wanted of her, and in a week or two she would go back to England and start all over again.

'You're thinking,' his voice was close in her ear, 'I can hear you. What's the matter?'

She schooled her voice to its usual quiet tones. 'Nothing—nothing at all. I expect I'm excited.'

'So am I. I wonder if it's about the same thing,' he added to puzzle her.

CHAPTER FIVE

THE flat, austere appearance of the house had not prepared her for the beauty within. The hall was long and narrow, widening at its end into two arches, beyond the right-hand one was a crimson-carpeted staircase, the left-hand arch revealed a door beyond it, presumably to the kitchen quarters. On the left of the marble-floored hall was a door, on the right there were double doors, arched and carved with swags of fruit and flowers, and still another door, similarly ornamented. There was little furniture, although it was beautiful enough—a wall table with a mirror above it and a bowl filled with tulips upon it, a chair, carved and straight-backed and cushioned with velvet, and a chandelier which gleamed and twinkled from the centre of the plastered ceiling.

Cassandra sighed with a mixture of happiness and sadness because she was going to love living here and because her stay was to be so short.

'How happy you must be to come home,' she said to the man beside her. 'I imagine that you know it all so well that it doesn't matter...'

'That I can't see? You're right. Home has a feeling about it, hasn't it?' His hand found her shoulder.

'Now I've been cruel, haven't I? The last thing I would wish to be with you, Cassandra.'

She was very conscious of his hand and her voice sounded rather small.

'It's quite all right, you know. I haven't had a home for quite a number of years now. When I've done my midwifery I shall find a small flat and make one...'

'Wouldn't you prefer Ogre's Relish?'

It would be nice to live there, but not very wise; it held too many memories. 'I should have to be near my work,' she told him seriously. 'Where do you wish to go?'

The hand tightened. 'First, you must meet Miep and then my aunt, and then we will have dinner.' He turned his head and said something to Miep who was helping Jan with the luggage, and she came over to them to take Cassandra's hand and welcome her with words which made no sense but which nonetheless held a warm welcome. For her own part she was only able to smile and stammer a little in English, which of course Miep couldn't understand, but they were friends instantly, and she felt thankful for that.

Jan had opened the pair of doors and Cassandra tucked her hand in Mr van Manfeld's arm and led him through them. The room they entered was a comfortable size, the walls panelled in white wood with an elaborate carved frame above the chimney-piece surrounding a landscape painting. The fireplace was of white marble with a brightly burning fire in its polished grate and on either side were winged armchairs. In the window was an enormous sofa, covered, as were the chairs, in needlework. Beside these, there were other, smaller chairs, together with a Pembroke table against one wall, holding some fine silver candlesticks and a great china bowl full of narcissi. There were small tables too, to hold the lamps which lighted the room, cream and a deep tawny orange which was the main colour of the tapestry covering the chairs. The carpet was of a dark blue design, as were the curtains. Cassandra, pausing on the threshold, thought it was one of the loveliest rooms she had ever seen, but there was no time to do more than give a quick look round her, for she was being urged forward to one of the wing chairs where sat an elderly lady.

'My aunt, Mevrouw van Manfeld,' said the ogre, pausing half-way across the room. 'She should be sitting on the right of the fire—she prefers that chair. How are you, my dear? And let me introduce Miss Cassandra Darling to you. She will be with us for a short time.'

He was by the chair by now and bent down, his hand outstretched, and the little lady took it and lifted her face to be kissed. 'Dear boy,' she said in excellent English, 'how very nice to see you again, and just in time for Sint Nicolaas too!' She turned to Cassandra, offered her a hand and said smilingly, 'It is delightful that Benedict has someone to bear him company through the next few days; he never listens to me, but I daresay he attends to you, my dear.'

Cassandra smiled. 'No, not really,' she answered, 'but Mr—Mijnheer van Manfeld needs someone to be his eyes just until he can leave off his dark glasses. Jan has been doing that until now, and wonderfully well. I can never hope to be so efficient, but I understand he...' she paused and Mevrouw van Manfeld continued for her, 'We've missed him dreadfully. Such an efficient man, as you say, he runs the place perfectly. We've missed you even more, Benedict, the house is dead without you. I've done all you asked me to attend to and I've told no one of your return as you wished, although Cornelius knows, of course, he'll be round presently. Now if you will tell me your wishes, Benedict—do you want to rest before dinner, or do you wish for something immediately?'

Her nephew had been standing quietly, letting her talk, a little smile around his mouth. Now he said: 'Oh, dinner at the usual time, I think, that will give us a chance to clean up. If Cornelius comes earlier, he can come up to my room—he'll stay for dinner of course. Jan can unpack my things and give me a hand and perhaps Miep will take Cassandra to her room.'

Cassandra said 'Yes, very well,' in her pleasant voice. She left him then, following Miep's ample proportions up the carved staircase to the floor above and across the landing to a small archway and two small steps, leading to a narrow passage at the back of the house. The door at its end opened on to a small, delightfully furnished bedroom with a bathroom leading out of it. Her case was already there, so she exchanged smiles with Miep, who sailed majestically away, leaving her to unpack.

No one had told her at what time dinner would be; she was debating the choice of going downstairs to see if there was anyone about, or remaining in her room until she was fetched, when there was a tap on the door and Jan came in.

'Mijnheer asked me to fetch you, Miss Cassandra,' he explained. 'Dinner is at eight o'clock, a little later than usual, but he would like you to come down for a drink first.'

Cassandra gave herself a last anxious look in the mirror and went to the door. 'Thank you, Jan, I was just wondering what I should do.' She smiled at him. 'I wanted to talk to you, just for a minute. I—I wanted you to know that I can't hope to take your place with Mijnheer van Manfeld—I'm only here for a short time.' She looked at him seriously. 'I feel as though I'd taken your job from you—I didn't intend…'

He interrupted her, his voice kind. 'You do not need to worry, Miss Cassandra. I would do anything for Mijnheer, anything, but I am glad to be back doing my own job, you understand. Someone had to be with him, to be his eyes and show him where to walk. And now there is the hope that he will see again for himself, but until then I am glad that it is you who is with him. He is anxious and on edge, you understand, not because he is afraid of being blind—he is never afraid, I think, but because he loves his work and life for him without it would be but half a life.' His black eyes studied hers. He went on slowly, 'He needs a wife, someone to love him and for him to love.'

Cassandra met the dark stare squarely. 'Is there anyone, Jan? Someone who could come if we let them know?'

He nodded, and her heart sank with the speed and weight of a stone into her neat suede shoes.

'There are plenty who would come most willingly, he has never lacked…but not with love, Miss Cassandra, only a love which thrives on good times and money spent upon them, a love which would turn to pity should his tests fail and later to something worse. But you are good for him, you do not listen to him when he shouts in anger, and you make him laugh.'

He was interrupted by his employer's voice, raised in a subdued roar wishing to know where everyone was. 'Come, Miss Cassandra,' Jan said urgently, and as an afterthought, 'You look pretty in that dress, if you do not mind me saying so.'

'No, of course I don't mind, Jan. I can do with plenty of encouragement.' They smiled at each other like a pair of conspirators and went downstairs.

Mijnheer van Manfeld was standing in the middle

of his hall, looking put out. At their approach he turned his head and remarked bitingly:

'So there you are—what kept you so long? You don't need to dress up, you know. Tante Beatrix thinks very little of modern fashion, Cornelius is more than middle-aged and I couldn't care less.'

Cassandra walked up to him, taking no notice of this piece of rudeness, whatever his opinion of her own appearance might be, she saw that he had changed into a superbly cut dark grey suit with a silk shirt and a tie of restrained richness. Quite the dandy.

'It wouldn't interest you to know that I dress to please myself.' She uttered this bare-faced lie in the measured tones of one not to be easily put out by other people's ill humour. 'Naturally I changed my dress after travelling for hours on end. I see you've done the same.' She smiled at the dark glasses. 'You look exactly what people expect a consultant to look like, I'm very tempted to call you sir.'

'God forbid! May I suggest that you call me Benedict?'

She said composedly, 'Yes, if you wish, but outside this house I shall address you as Mijnheer van Manfeld.'

He shrugged his shoulders. 'As you wish. Shall we have a drink while we wait for Tante Beatrix?'

She agreed to sherry and watched him make his way across the room to the table between the windows, upon which stood a massive silver tray holding decanters and glasses. They were obviously in a well-remembered order; almost without fumbling he poured her drink, gave himself a whisky and crossed the room again, the drinks balanced in one hand, the stick in the other.

'How long were you at home before you went to Mull?' she asked.

'Three weeks—a little more. Time for me to learn my way around my own house. Not so difficult, for everything was kept in exactly the same place and as I was born and brought up here, it was easy to remember. It wasn't so easy in the cottage, it was so small.'

She sipped her sherry and found it good. 'Is it your cottage?'

'No. Cornelius—my partner—had an English wife—she is dead now—who inherited the place from some Scottish relative. They used to go there a great deal, but now he doesn't care to. It seemed an ideal place for me to go to.' He paused as the front door bell rang and a moment later there were voices in the hall. 'Cornelius,' said Mijnheer van Manfeld with satisfaction.

The man who came into the room was middle-aged, tall and burly, with a large, rugged face, a blunt nose and grey hair. As he came in he shot a penetrating look at Cassandra and said in excellent English,

'Benedict—it's good to see you, *jongen*!' He shook the hand his partner held out as he got up.

'Cassandra,' said Benedict, 'this is my partner,

Cornelius van Tromp. Cor—Miss Cassandra Darling, and I must warn you not to attempt any jokes about her name.'

Cassandra shook hands, conscious that she was being closely scrutinized. She thought that Mijnheer van Tromp looked a sweetie—she could imagine that they would work very well in partnership.

'Help yourself to a drink,' Benedict said, 'and tell us all your news.'

'You mean when have I arranged for you to see Viske in Utrecht? Two days' time—no hope of anything sooner with Sint Nicolaas so close. Nine o'clock at the Sint Paulus Ziekenhuis, then again in the afternoon if it's thought necessary—X-rays, check up on general health and so on, you know it all. If everything is satisfactory you will be able to throw away those blinkers. Homatrophine drops the night before, but Nurse will see to that.'

He smiled at her as he spoke and asked, 'May I call you Cassandra? Nurse is so stiff.'

Cassandra smiled gratefully at him. 'Yes, please do, Mijnheer van Tromp.' She glanced quickly at Benedict because it was hard not to, and found him faintly smiling. He had sat down in one of the armchairs beside the fire and his partner had taken a chair between them.

'You'll spend Sint Nicolaas with us, Cornelius?' Benedict invited.

'May I? Some time after tea—that will be delightful.' He turned to Cassandra. 'I live close by, you know. Like Benedict I have a consulting room attached to my house, though I do far less surgery than he does, and very little hospital work—I leave that to him. I understand that you have had good experience in theatre?'

She told him swiftly. He nodded when she had finished and said to Benedict, 'Did I tell you that Lulu is leaving me shortly? She is going to Australia to live with her sister.'

Benedict's dark glasses exchanged a long thoughtful stare with his partner. 'No,' he said at length, 'you didn't tell me,' and changed the subject abruptly.

After dinner they went back to the sitting-room and the talk was wholly of the forthcoming festivities. 'A pity we shall be so quiet this year,' Mijnheer van Manfeld told Cassandra. 'Usually we have a house full of guests. This year there will be nothing, I'm afraid; it will be the quietest of evenings, for I am under oath to do nothing much until Viske has seen me—he'll have my head if I don't.'

Cassandra overcame a strong urge to go to a party with the ogre. 'Oh well,' she said comfortably, 'you can make up for it by having an extra large party next year—think how you will enjoy that.'

'You consider me a party-loving man, Cassandra?' His voice was silky and she gave him a suspicious glance; she had heard that tone before.

'I haven't considered you at all,' she answered untruthfully, and saw his faint mocking smile; he was going to bait her... In her most agreeable voice she said: 'Would you mind if I went to bed? It's been such an exciting day.'

'Certainly. Good night, Cassandra. Eight o'clock in the morning in my room, if you please.'

'Very well. Good night, Mevrouw van Manfeld and Mijnheer van Tromp.' She shook hands with them because they seemed to expect it, perhaps it was a Dutch custom, although Benedict made no move to do so, merely stood. In two days he would be able to see her. She wondered, briefly, what he would say, and as she left the room and crossed the hall, she longed for a fairy godmother who would wave her wand and turn her into a beauty of such magnificence that Benedict would be struck speechless.

She was up betimes in the morning, and at exactly eight o'clock made her way across the landing to her patient's room which Jan had thoughtfully pointed out to her on the previous evening. She looked neat in her white uniform, her slim waist encircled by the dark blue belt with its elaborate silver buckle, not a hair out of place beneath the old-fashioned cap with its starched streamers. The room she entered after a brisk knock was darkened by the heavy curtains at its windows, the bed empty. Benedict was sitting in an armchair with its back to any light which might creep in from the early morning outside. Despite the gloom she thought the room must, in a proper light, be a very fine one, several times larger than her own and furnished with furniture massive enough to suit the occupier. He sat very still, looking, even in the dimness, quite different without his glasses; more approachable, much more to be loved. She brushed aside the thought, wished him a friendly good morning and on his quiet instructions, went to the adjoining bathroom, shutting the door carefully first before putting on the light. His eye-drops were on the bathroom shelf. Cassandra read the label carefully, picked up the kidney dish, the towel, the pipette, the undine and the sterile water, turned off the light and went back into the bedroom. It pleased her that he hadn't questioned her at all—offered no doubt as to whether she had the correct bottle and everything which went with it; at least he trusted her.

His voice was quiet. 'Wait—I'll need another chair so that you can get at me. There's a small straight one by the writing table.'

She hadn't expected him to be a good patient, she had thought he would be impatient of the finicky little business of washing out his eyes, putting in the drops; but he sat very still, his fine head tilted backwards while she performed her task meticulously. It was unnerving to look down, even in that gloom, into his eyes, even though she knew that he could see her only as a shadowy figure, in the even more shadowed room. When she had finished she gave him his dark glasses and asked:

'Shall I fetch Jan?'

'Please, and thank you, Cassandra. We shall meet

at breakfast.' It was gentle dismissal; presumably she cleared up her paraphernalia when he had dressed.

They were half-way through breakfast when he told her, 'I should like to go shopping, and you will accompany me, if you please. Jan will drive. Have you a cloak? No matter, there is one in my surgery, my nurse left hers and she won't be back until the New Year.' He turned his head and called, 'Jan?' and when he came spoke to him in Dutch and presently he came back to tell her that the cloak was in her bedroom.

She was glad to find that it was exactly like her own hospital cloak had been, navy blue with a warm scarlet lining. She put it on and went downstairs to find the master of the house.

She guided him through the door and outside to where Jan was waiting with the car—not the Aston Martin, she noted with surprise, but a Daimler Sovereign. Jan opened the door for her and she got in, and Benedict, after a few words with Jan, got in beside her.

When he had settled himself he remarked affably, 'I can hear you wondering.'

'Then you can tell me without waiting for me to ask,' she added, 'Mijnheer van Manfeld,' a little coldly.

He grinned. 'And what have I done that we should suddenly be on such frigid terms?' he wanted to know. 'I thought I was Benedict.'

'Well, Benedict, then. I expected the Aston Martin, that was all.'

'And with commendable restraint, made no comment upon your expectations. I find this car better in the town—besides, it's most suitable for my profession, don't you think?'

He was making fun of her, and when he laughed she laughed too and conceded, 'It's a lovely car. Where are we going?'

'Just to the shops in Rhenen—only a minute or so's drive. Jan has a list of things he has written down and I want you to buy them.'

'Me?' She was appalled. 'I can't buy anything, I can't understand a word!'

'You won't need to. Just go inside the shops and hand over the list and pay with the money I shall give you. It will be an excellent exercise for you.'

Cassandra was doubtful, but it worked better than she had anticipated. She spoke no word, merely handed over the slip of paper, received the packages and paid with the notes Benedict gave her. She even began to enjoy herself, and when she came out of the third shop, her arms full of gaily wrapped packages, she observed, 'I wish I knew what I was buying, it would be so much more fun.'

'Certainly you are not to know. That's the lot, I think.'

She was standing at the car's door ready to get in again when she became aware that there was someone behind her, and a charming voice, speaking

Dutch with the faintest trace of a lisp, addressed Benedict. Cassandra looked round; the owner of the voice certainly had a fairy godmother; no one else could have given her such bright blue eyes with such curling lashes, such a small straight nose and lovely mouth. Her hair, cropped short under a pert little fur cap, was the colour of corn at harvest time and she was as tall as Cassandra, who looked quickly at Benedict and for one brief second was sure that he wasn't in the least pleased at the advent of this beautiful creature—but she must have imagined it, for his rather sternly set mouth broke into a smile and he turned his face towards her voice with every appearance of pleasure. The girl said something else and this time Benedict spoke in English.

'Nurse, if you would be so good as to sit in front, this young lady will be coming back to the house with us.'

For the short journey back, Cassandra tried to make up her mind who the girl could be. An old friend, for he had recognized her voice at once—a girl-friend—*the* girl-friend, perhaps. It was bound to happen, she had known that, but it didn't make it any easier now that it had. She got out at the house and was immediately arrested by Benedict's voice asking her quite sharply to go with him to the sitting-room. She helped him into the house as unobtrusively as possible, considerably hampered by the fair beauty who hovered round them in a useless fashion, getting in the way in her efforts to stay close to Benedict.

Once in the sitting-room, Jan took his master's coat and disappeared and Cassandra, with a muttered, 'You won't want me for a little while, Mijnheer van Manfeld,' made for the door, to be halted by his bland request to remain where she was.

'You must meet my nurse,' he told his visitor, 'Miss Cassandra Darling, and this, Cassandra, is an old friend, Juffrouw van der Plas.'

There was nothing in his voice to indicate his feelings, but Cassandra felt sure that he must be in love with the silly lovely creature, and she couldn't blame him if he was. She shook hands with the girl and stayed by the door until Benedict turned his head and said irritably, 'You're still waiting to go, then?' In Mull she would have answered him back, but not now. She went to the kitchen to talk to Jan.

Jan was arranging his parcels neatly on the kitchen table, and although he gave her a surprised look, he didn't speak, so that she felt forced to say, 'Jan, should I have stayed? She seemed such a—a close friend.' She added defiantly as though he had argued with her, 'He didn't want me to.'

He gave her one of his dark looks. 'Oh, yes, he did, Miss Cassandra, that's why you're here, isn't it? To be his dragon and keep his well-meaning friends at arm's length. It was bad luck meeting Juffrouw van der Plas like that—the last we heard of her, she was in America.'

'Oh—is she, was she...I had the impression that they knew each other rather well.'

Jan smiled briefly. 'I'm not one to gossip, Miss Cassandra, but seeing that it's you—this young lady has had her elegant claws in Mijnheer for quite a time, with no good result, I can tell you that. Perhaps at first he liked her, she's pretty enough if you like the vapid type, but Mijnheer has never had serious thought about her, you understand.'

Cassandra had listened quietly. 'All right, Jan, I'll go back. I'll think of some excuse…you're sure?'

She could hear Juffrouw van der Plas' pretty voice prattling away as she crossed the hall again; she seemed to have a lot to say and she was laughing a great deal too. Cassandra opened the double doors and said the first thing which entered her head in as convincing a tone as she could manage.

'Your eye treatment, Mijnheer van Manfeld.' She spoke severely. 'It's due now. I'm sorry to interrupt…' Her voice sounded as starched as her uniform. Impossible to read the expression on that spectacled face turned towards her—fury, relief, amusement? She would soon know. She waited quietly while he explained in his own incomprehensible language, while good-byes were said, while his lovely visitor went to the great mirror over the wall table and adjusted her jaunty cap to a still jauntier angle and at last went away with Jan, who had appeared silently to open the front door.

'Come in and shut the door,' ordered the ogre in a nasty voice, 'and be good enough to explain why you deserted me.'

'I did no such thing!' said Cassandra indignantly.
'If you imagine that I was going to stand by, playing
gooseberry...'

'Gooseberry? What is this talk of gooseberry—a
distasteful fruit, all skin and pips.'

'It's an expression, and with your knowledge of
English you must know very well what it means.'

'Whether I have or not I will leave you to guess.'
He asked suavely, 'Did you find Juffrouw van der
Plas pretty?'

'She's beautiful.'

'Yes, she is. An ornament to society, one might
say.' He beamed at her. 'I had no idea that you could
lie so convincingly,' he told her with interest.

Cassandra went a delicate pink. 'I don't make a
habit of it,' her voice was stiff, 'but it was in a good
cause, at least I hope it was.'

'Dear girl, I am glad to see that you take your
duties so seriously. Come here.'

She advanced with some hesitation until she was
standing beside his chair, and when he put out a
hand, she placed hers in it. 'Don't do that again,' he
begged her, 'don't leave me alone; don't force me to
listen to girls tinkling on about the parties I missed.'
He smiled and turned his head towards her and Cassandra, standing very straight before him, longed to
throw her arms around his neck and tell him that she
would never leave him again, he had only to say the
word... 'You see,' he went on, 'it was like meeting
someone from another world, one I've grown out of.

I almost lost my temper, but I saved it to wreak on you. I don't know about the rest of you, Cassandra, but I'm sure you have broad shoulders.'

'I don't mind when you lose your temper,' she said in a little voice, then caught her breath as he lifted her hand and kissed it gently.

'No?' He gave her back the hand and she put it behind her back, out of temptation's way, and said in as matter-of-fact voice as she could manage, 'What do you want done with the things you bought?'

He grinned. 'Curious to know? Jan will see to them. Shall we go out this afternoon? Tante Beatrix likes to rest after lunch and Jan will be busy. You shall drive the car.'

She was appalled. 'Oh, I couldn't—it's on the wrong side of the road, and supposing I bumped into something?'

'Regrettable, but unlikely; your brother-in-law told me that you were a good driver, so don't let us have any prissy nonsense. We'll take the Daimler and go up towards the Veluwe and you can describe the scenery to me as we go. I shall enjoy it.' He sounded smug.

'Well, all right, but I don't suppose I shall.'

'And wear your uniform, dear girl.'

She looked at him in sheer astonishment. 'But— but I'll look silly, driving a car in a cape.' She frowned. 'Why?'

'Not silly, rather fetching, I should imagine. And

just stop to think, Cassandra Darling. A great many people know me, you understand. It's one thing to be accompanied by a nurse, quite another if my companion is a young lady.'

Her charming bosom swelled with the strength of her feelings. 'Well,' she ejaculated, 'what a rude thing to say! I suppose you're thinking of your reputation?'

The dark glasses conveyed amused contempt. 'Mine? No, young lady, yours.'

She said 'Oh,' and nothing else, for there was nothing else to say, and he must have realized this because presently he said, 'Exactly,' in a final, satisfied way. He got up. 'Shall we have a drink? Tante Beatrix will be here in a few minutes; she enjoys a glass of sherry before lunch.'

They started off under a cold grey sky. Jan had brought the car round to the front door and Cassandra, getting behind the wheel in some trepidation, was relieved to find that once she was there, it wasn't too bad. It was even better when Benedict, beside her, said:

'I don't know what you're getting so excited about. I'm here, aren't I?'

It was ridiculous to feel quite safe just because he was. After all, what could he do in a moment of crisis? She said severely, 'You're not to take your glasses off whatever happens,' and was rewarded by his bellow of laughter.

She drove cautiously out of the little town, follow-

ing the not too busy road to Wageringen, and then
at her companion's direction, turning off to go to
Ede, and then on to Otterlo in the Hoge Veluwe Park,
where, Benedict informed her, there was a splendid
collection of paintings which she really would have
to visit some time. A mere figure of speech, she decided, for she could envisage no days off during her
brief stay in Holland.

She was beginning to enjoy herself; the car was a
delight to drive, Benedict an even greater delight to
be with. She did her best to describe the country they
passed through, and in return he told her titbits of
history and anecdotes about the villages and houses
they passed. A few miles beyond Otterlo he told her
to turn off on to the road to Barneveld.

'There's another road back to Rhenen, just as
pretty, and a rather good castle,' he explained, and
entertained her with more tales as they drove through
the flat peaceful countryside, the dusk already creeping towards them. They reached the castle, paused
briefly while he told her a little about it, and drove
on again. Soon the lights of Rhenen greeted them
again, very gay and festive because in an hour or so
Sint Nicolaas with his black attendant, Zwarte Piet,
would be visiting every house in Holland, leaving
presents for the good children and reading the riot
act to the naughty ones. Cassandra, listening to a
detailed account of this national event, commented:
'So no one knows who gives the presents. They all,
presumably, come from Sint Nicolaas?'

'That's right, and of course no one must tell anyone else who has given what.'

'It's for the children?'

'Of course, but that doesn't prevent grown-up people giving each other presents. It's a splendid opportunity, because it's quite admissible to give gifts and pass it off as coming from Sint Nicolaas.'

'Oh—I imagine a popular girl gets snowed under.'

'Naturally. Turn left here and then right at the crossroads and then left again.'

They were home. She drew up outside the house, switched off the engine and opened her door.

'So you did enjoy it after all?' He sounded faintly mocking.

'Yes, very much, and it passed the afternoon for you.'

The corners of his mouth twitched. 'As you say, Cassandra, the afternoon has been passed. Let us go indoors.'

They had tea with Tante Beatrix, holding a mild conversation which was presently interrupted by the arrival of Mijnheer van Tromp, who refused the offer of a fresh made pot of tea, wished everyone a hearty good day, expressed admiration for Cassandra's cap, and sat himself down by the fire.

'It will snow before the week's out,' he informed them cheerfully. 'With luck, Benedict, you may get some skating. Do you skate, Cassandra?'

She had to admit that she didn't. 'I haven't a clue. It looks so easy but I'm sure it's not.'

'As easy as walking once you've got your balance. An hour between Benedict and me and you'll be off like a bird, no holding you.'

'How simple you make it sound! I…' she came to an abrupt halt because of the thunderous knocking on the front door. She looked at the three faces turned towards her, her mouth open, and before she could speak:

'Sint Nicolaas,' Benedict told her quite seriously. 'It's about this time he comes. Be good enough to go to the door and see if he has left anything.'

She went obediently, caught up in the childish magic of the legend and not in the least surprised, therefore, to find an enormous sack in the front porch. She was peering at it with excited interest when Jan appeared.

'Ah, Sint Nicolaas has been,' he remarked in much the same tones he might have used to tell her that the postman had been. 'I'll carry this in for you, Miss Cassandra.'

Which he did, to be greeted by Benedict's 'I told you so,' his partner's 'I wonder what I've got this year,' and Tante Beatrix' happy twitterings.

It was tremendous fun, for everyone had several gifts, gaily wrapped and extravagantly beribboned and all of them bearing the words: from Sint Nicolaas. It took quite a long time to hand them round, an undertaking Cassandra had been asked to accept, while Miep and Jan, who had joined them, handed round champagne and passed little dishes of nuts and sugared fruit and small cheesy biscuits. But at last she had emptied the sack, to sit back on her heels, like an excited little girl while, one by one, they each opened their presents.

She was a little overwhelmed because her presents were unexpected. She knew now what was in the square boxes she had carried so carefully to the car that morning. Chocolate letters, the initials of the recipients; she had one, like everyone else. She had handkerchiefs too, and a little round fur cap, and a ridiculous china animal which looked vaguely like a kitten. There was French soap too, and chocolates, and an outsize bottle of Dioressence. Cassandra thanked the saint suitably, her eyes on Mijnheer van Manfeld, staring blandly before him into his navy blue space.

They dined, then went back to the sitting-room afterwards and had coffee and more conversation, none of which she remembered later on when she was in bed. But it had been a lovely day; she doubted if there would be another like it; tomorrow, her ogre would be able to see again—she was sure of that, and nothing would be the same after that, because he would take one look at her and, however polite he was, she would see the faint amused smile; much the same look as she had once surprised on the face of the young Registrar she had imagined she was in love with so long ago—in another world, because it hadn't contained Benedict.

They made an early start in a morning which was

both cold and dark. She went, as neat as a new pin, to put the drops in Benedict's eyes, and because he was silent save for a good morning, Cassandra stayed silent too, knowing how he felt. Over breakfast, though, he carried on a conversation which touched on every subject save one—himself, and she, giving polite answers to his observations, longed to be back in Ogre's Relish, listening to some tirade or other and feeling justified in answering him back. But not now. It was a relief when they got up from the table and Benedict said, 'Jan is coming with us.'

Cassandra handed him his stick. 'Yes, of course. I supposed he would.'

'Why of course?' he snapped, 'or have you already made my arrangements for me?'

He was edgy, but then so would she have been in like circumstances.

'You know I haven't, but he's been with you—looked after you constantly. He has every right to share in your happiness.'

'Yes. You have a sharp mind, Miss Darling, and a boundless optimism which I hope will be justified before the day is out.'

'It will, and it's not optimism, it's faith.'

They were in the hall by now and Jan and Miep were there, watching them. Mijnheer van Manfeld put out a hand and touched her arm. 'Whatever it is, will you wish me luck, Cassandra?' His voice was almost humble.

She didn't mind Miep and Jan being there. She

stretched up and kissed him warmly on the cheek.
'You know I wish you that,' she said steadily.

They went in the Aston Martin, with Jan driving,
and once they were clear of Rhenen he drove very
fast, sensing that it suited his employer's mood. Benedict didn't have a great deal to say; he explained a
little about the hospital they were going to, but first
they would go to the ophthalmologist's own house
for the lengthy examinations, then later to the hospital for the X-rays. Then, with any luck, there might
be a cautious opinion and the return home; on the
other hand... It would be enough to try the patience
of a saint, and Benedict was hardly that. Cassandra
put out her hand and tucked it into Benedict's while
the sensible side of her brain told her that she was
being a fool to do it. But apparently she wasn't; his
fingers closed round hers with a firm grip and although he said nothing, she saw him smile.

Utrecht seemed vast and bustling and noisy after
Rhenen. The specialist lived in the heart of the city,
in a narrow house overlooking the Oudegracht. The
street teemed with people and traffic, but once they
were behind the great front door they seemed to be
in another world of peace and quiet and subdued col-
ours. Mijnheer Viske lived there too. His consulting
rooms were on the ground floor and they were ushered immediately into the waiting room, where Jan
sat down without fuss and Cassandra, uncertain, hovered behind her patient, almost hidden by his broad
back. But Mijnheer Viske, small, rotund and jolly,

seemed to take it for granted that she would go into the consulting room too. Only when they were in it, with Benedict in a chair facing the enormous desk, did he say:

'Viske, this is Miss Cassandra Darling, who very kindly came back with me to help me over the journey and settle in. She's able to cope.'

The little man nodded, smiled and said in English, 'Hullo, Nurse. We shall begin with a little talk—in Dutch. Please sit until I am ready for you.'

She sat, listening to the little man talking. He had a pleasant voice, quiet and a little monotonous; she suspected that he had trained himself to speak like that; people without sight would be liable to get fussed with too much heartiness. He talked for some time and Benedict, sitting quietly, said nothing at all, but presently she was able to see that the actual examination was beginning, for Mijnheer was asking questions and Benedict was answering them. He did so without haste and with a calm she could sense was quite unforced. After a little while, the specialist said in English, 'So far, so good. Now we go to the darkroom. Be good enough to follow, Nurse.'

The examination room was behind the desk, through a little door cut in the wall. Cassandra settled Benedict in a chair and at a nod from Mijnheer Viske took up her position at a small table nearby. The ophthalmologist adjusted the slit lamp which he would use later, nodded to her to pass him the ophthalmoscope, and began to examine his patient's

eyes, each in turn, and at great length. He muttered
to himself, and sometimes to his patient while he was
doing this, but Cassandra, straining her ears, could
make no sense of anything he said. At length he finished, had a short conversation with Benedict and
proceeded to the second phase; the optical examination for the estimation of refraction errors. This
test, it transpired, was entirely satisfactory. The two
men murmured together and laughed a little, and
Cassandra, eaten up with anxiety, wondered how
they could as, at the specialist's request, she adjusted
the Bjerrum screen so that he could examine the field
of vision. He was, as befitted one of the finest eye
specialists in Europe, a thorough man. He took his
time over this too and when he had finished, had
quite a lot to say to Benedict, but at last he said,
'The slit lamp, if you please, Nurse.'

This last and final examination was more compli-
cated by reason of the various attachments he re-
quired her to put on and take off from time to time.
It was lengthy too, and he whiled away the time with
inconsequential chat between his bouts of deep concentration when peering into his patient's eyes. It
seemed an age before he said:

'So—enough is enough. Now the X-rays, Benedict. They will see to those at once, naturally. I am
not going to commit myself—if I did I would quickly
lose all my patients, eh?' he shook with laughter at
the very idea, 'but I believe that your sight is fully
restored. Care, of course; tinted glasses; no operating

for a week or so, naturally. The drops each morning, too, but these little nuisances can be borne, can they not? Tomorrow, when you come, we will do the estimation of colour vision.'

He caught Benedict's hand and shook it. 'I am very happy for you, but I must beg of you to take care, the smallest thing might jeopardize a total cure. No gay life for a little while, a little work if you must, but early nights, a quiet chat—you know what I mean. To drive the car will not hurt as long as it is done in moderation, but only after we have consulted the X-rays.'

He looked at the silent man beside him. 'And still a few days before you start work, van Manfeld. You have to get used to using your eyes once more.'

Benedict stirred in his chair. 'Everything you say, Viske, and many thanks. There is just one thing. I want to look at Cassandra.'

If Mijnheer Viske found this request in any way unusual, he made no sign. 'Why not? Nurse, will you come over here and I will shine the lamp on you. Not too bright, I think, and only for a very short time.'

She stood miserably, aware that her sharp little nose would look even sharper in the lamp's rays, and that her mouth was widening into the size of a letterbox. She gazed obediently in front of her, towards the gloom where Benedict sat, and heaved an audible sigh of relief when the lamp was switched off.

'Not long enough,' said Benedict softly.

'Yes, it was.' She knew her voice sounded waspish. 'Long enough for you to see that I was right.'

'Right?'

'I told you that I was plain.'

'So you did. The lamp must flatter you. That's a ridiculous cap.'

She said stiffly, 'It's my hospital cap. I'm proud of it.'

He laughed. 'Never mind, it suits you. I shall take a longer, more critical look when I have my new glasses.'

So her cap was ridiculous and it suited her. Did that mean that he found her ridiculous too? She handed him his stick without a word, and followed the two men back into the waiting room.

There was a brief delay there while Jan was told the news. His strange craggy face was lit by a smile of delight. He wrung Mijnheer van Manfeld's hand, saying a great deal in Dutch, so that Cassandra couldn't understand a word, but presently he turned to her and said, 'A great moment, Miss Cassandra. We must not be too hasty, eh? But what news! I am a happy man.'

She smiled at him, liking him very much. 'I'm sure you are, Jan, for I'm sure that it was your help that made all those tedious weeks bearable. We have to go to the hospital, I believe.'

There was no waiting about when they arrived there—indeed, there was a reception committee which whisked him discreetly through endless cor-

ridors, with Cassandra pattering along behind until
he spoke to one of the men beside him, who detached
himself from the main party and fell back to walk
with her, chatting pleasantly in an English as good
as her own.

'We shall be glad when Professor van Manfeld
returns,' he told her.

'Oh, is he a professor?' she wanted to know, thinking at the same time how little she knew about Benedict. 'I'm sure you will, and he will be glad to come
back, I know.'

She glanced at the broad back in its impeccably
cut grey suiting, walking ahead of her along corridors
which he most likely knew blindfold; walking away
from her. The thought was unendurable. She turned
to her companion and asked brightly, 'How many
beds do you have here?' and made herself listen
while he told her.

CHAPTER SIX

THE X-rays were quickly done, but the get-together in the radiologist's office afterwards went on for some time. Cassandra had been feeling a little lost until Jan arrived. He had crossed the room to her side as soon as he had seen her. 'Mijnheer sent for me,' he explained. 'I am to take coffee here.'

She glanced over to where Benedict stood talking to the radiologist and several other men—colleagues at the hospital, she guessed, for they all wore the same conventional suits, the same elegant ties.

'That was nice of him,' she murmured. 'He wants you to share in his good news.'

Jan's dark eyes rested upon hers for a moment, but before he could speak he was summoned by Benedict's quiet 'Jan?' and left her with an apologetic smile. She watched him being introduced to the other men and thought how like Mijnheer van Manfeld to give credit where credit was due—she deliberately called him that to herself; it would help to prise her loose from the silly situation she had allowed herself to get into. Nevertheless, when he turned his head and said 'Cassandra?' she went to him at once, to be introduced in her turn. But presently she slipped to the edge of the circle of people around him and Jan joined her with her coffee cup in his hand, remarking, 'It is all so strange, is it not, Miss Cassandra, but it is a wonderful hour for Mijnheer.'

She sipped her coffee. 'Yes, it is. How proud you must be of your part in getting him well again.' She looked at Benedict, standing with downbent head, listening to someone or other. 'Thank you, Jan,' she said softly.

'Do not thank me, I am only glad that I could at last repay some of the kindness I have received from Mijnheer. He needed my help, just as he needs the love you give him, Miss Cassandra.'

She stared at his dark, elderly face, the blood leaving her own and then rushing back to flood it from her chin to the roots of her neat hair. She whispered, 'Oh, Jan, he doesn't know? He mustn't—how did you…? I thought I'd been so careful…'

He gave her a slow reassuring smile. 'Do not worry, it is not to be seen, only to be felt, you understand. It is a secret which I share with you, and I am proud to do that.' He sighed. 'If things had been different, I would have had a daughter of just your age, Miss Cassandra.'

She forgot her own miserable embarrassment in the sadness of his face. 'I've often wondered. Would you tell me about her one day?'

He nodded. 'I should like that. I do not talk of it, you understand, only Mijnheer knows, but I should like to tell you too, about her and my wife…' He broke off as Benedict called: 'Jan, come here a moment, will you? There's something…and where's Cassandra?' He turned his head sharply, frowning.

'I'm here,' she told him quietly, 'with Jan,' and stayed where she was until he said decisively: 'Please come here—I'm sorry, I didn't realize you weren't with us.'

She went and joined the little group, making conversation and listening to Benedict's voice and, now and again, his laugh. He hadn't laughed so much in all the time she had known him. He must be overjoyed to return to his own life and his friends once more. She was jerked out of her thoughts by her patient's voice, requesting her to give him an arm back to the car. There was a little flurry of good-byes and 'see you tomorrows' and they set off, this time alone, because Jan had gone on ahead.

'Is there anyone about?' Benedict wanted to know. Cassandra peered behind her, in front of her and even sideways at the blank walls on either side of them. 'No,' she said at length.

He said disconcertingly, 'Cassandra, you know how happy I am, don't you?'

'Of course I know. I'm happy too and so is Jan, and so will Penny and Andrew be happy when I tell them, and everyone else who knows you.'

'You minded me looking at you at Viske's, didn't you?'

She lied briskly, 'No, why should I? I—I told you that I was a plain girl so that I knew that it wouldn't be too much of a shock to you.'

He said simply, 'It was a great shock. I—Is there someone coming?'

She looked behind her. 'Yes, your partner.'

'Cornelius? Damn!' They stood waiting for him to catch up with them and then went on together, but now Mijnheer van Tromp had Benedict's arm, talking urgently in Dutch, and Cassandra walked sedately beside them, wrapped in her own thoughts. So he had had a shock, had he? Hadn't he believed her, then? She had been quite honest and told him that she was plain; what more could she have done? Perhaps he had thought that she was playing some pleasant little joke. Her too-sharp nose wrinkled at the absurdity of it.

They were at the entrance before Benedict said to her, 'Forgive us, Cassandra, this was a little urgent business which couldn't be postponed.' He shook hands with his partner, just as though he wouldn't see him again for days—a silly custom, she thought crossly, shaking everyone by the hand on every possible occasion. All the same she smiled as she took Mijnheer van Tromp's hand when he offered it; he was nice, she liked him better each time she saw him.

They travelled back as fast as they had come, with Jan singing a little song under his breath and Benedict sitting silent. And this time she kept her hands folded primly on her lap.

At the house, Benedict paused to say, 'Tomorrow again, then. My new glasses should be ready by then—if everything is all right, I shall put them on and drive the car back myself. You will both come with me of course.'

They went up the three steps to the already opened door, where Miep was waiting and who, on being told the news, burst into a flood of happy tears so that Benedict had to pat her enormous shoulders to quiet her. 'Champagne tomorrow when I get back,' he told her. 'I think it's a little previous to have it today, don't you? Where's my aunt?'

At lunch Benedict was polite but a little absent-minded. No doubt he was making plans, Cassandra decided, pecking at the delicious food on her plate. She was quite startled when he asked her if she would read some extracts from *The Lancet* and *World Medicine* to him that afternoon.

'Even when I leave off these dark glasses,' he explained, 'Viske won't hear of me reading for more than half an hour or so a day to start with, so I must cram in as much as I can.'

'Before I go,' added Cassandra silently as she agreed cheerfully to do as he asked.

She was half way through a particularly dry article on Henoch's Purpura when there was a knock on the door and the beautiful Juffrouw van der Plas swept in, exquisitely groomed, very sure of her welcome and towing a companion. Another pretty girl, Cassandra saw with a sinking heart, blonde too, her hair falling round her shoulders, her suede, fur-trimmed jacket, gaily embroidered, pulled tight over suede slacks stuffed into high boots. She was hung with chains and bracelets which tinkled with every movement she made. They played a positive tune as she raced across the room, flung her arms round Benedict's neck and kissed him, and her companion, not to be outdone, did the same. Cassandra, watching silently, knew that he was annoyed and she made a little movement so that Juffrouw van der Plas turned to look at her—a kind look, such as she would have given a small child or a puppy or anything else which was to be vaguely noticed. Cassandra took instant exception to it; it would have been nice if she could have said what was on her mind. Instead she asked coldly:

'Am I to remain, Mijnheer van Manfeld?'

'Yes, of course.' His voice was sharp. 'You will stay exactly where you are.' He took no further notice of her but said something at some length to the two girls, who looked bewildered, faintly amused and slightly regretful. Cassandra was surprised when they got up, shook him by the hand, smiled at her— quite differently this time, she didn't fail to notice— and went away.

When the front door had clanged shut after them she got to her feet.

'Shall I wipe the lipstick off your face, Mijnheer van Manfeld?' she asked, very coldly.

'For God's sake, yes—and stop calling me Mijnheer van Manfeld with every other breath.'

She went and stood before him and got out her handkerchief, said briefly: 'Put out your tongue,' damped her handkerchief and scrubbed the offending marks away. By the time she had finished he was shaking with laughter.

'And now what's the matter?' she wanted to know.

But he refused to tell her, merely shaking his head, so that she observed crossly, 'I can't think why you couldn't have spent an hour or so with your friends. After all, they were kind enough to come and see you…!'

'They came because they had heard that I'm—er—normal again. Do you suppose they would have bothered if I were to remain blind?' He lifted a lazy hand and caught hers. 'Do you know,' he said slowly, 'I think my tastes have changed—in people, I mean—and it is your doing, Cassandra.' He put up his other hand and took off his dark glasses and when she said, 'No—you mustn't—Mijnheer Viske said…' said, 'Be quiet, dear girl.'

She stood like a slender statue, staring into his eyes. They were grey and searching; under their gaze she felt her colour rise slowly until her face was flooded with a delicate pinkness. She whispered:

'Oh, please—you shouldn't! He said not…supposing it should do harm? And after all these weeks.'

He smiled. 'The harm's done, Cassandra, if that is what you call it. Why did you tell me that you were plain?'

She pulled her hand away. 'Well, I am,' she mumbled.

It would have been so nice if he had denied this hotly, instead he put his glasses on again with a little laugh and said: 'Would you mind finishing the article—the interruption was pleasant enough, but ill-timed.'

She picked up *The Lancet* and found her place. 'They are two of the prettiest girls I've seen,' she assured him, 'and if I'd been you I would have thrown *The Lancet* into the waste paper basket and asked them to stay for tea.'

'Yes?' He sounded amused and his face was bland. 'But you see I can have the pleasure of seeing any of my friends whenever I wish, but I fear that none of them are capable of reading about Henoch's Purpura with any degree of intelligence, and you are, Cassandra.'

She read the rest of the article in a prim voice, stopping and re-reading bits of it when he asked her to do so, and when she had finished he thanked her pleasantly.

'And where will you spend Christmas?' His question was such a surprise that she dropped *The Lancet*.

'With Rachel, I suppose.'

'You look forward to that?' his voice was hatefully silky, she wondered what he would say next, she hadn't long to wait. 'An excellent opportunity to become better acquainted with John Campbell,' was what he said.

'I have no wish...' she began crossly, and then

changed it to: 'I doubt if there'll be much time; clergymen are notoriously busy at Christmastime.'

His voice became even silkier, and she saw that he was smiling. 'Do you not have a saying in your language—"Love will find a way"?'

She got to her feet, 'You're being most unpleasant,' she told him. 'I'm sure I don't know why. There's no point in me sitting here while you think up nasty remarks to needle me. There is,' she went on, a little breathless, 'no point in my remaining here, in Holland—you won't need a nurse now and you have friends enough to entertain you and give you any help you may need.'

He was standing too. 'So I have,' he agreed smoothly, 'and you are quite right, I shall have no further need of you as a nurse after tomorrow.'

Cassandra felt wretched; she had known that he would tell her that she was no longer needed, but she need not have precipitated it. She reached the door and took hold of its brass knob, where it was instantly held fast by his own hand. He had moved with lightning speed and now he loomed over her, standing relaxed, almost lazily, though his hand was firm enough on hers. He had taken off his dark glasses again, too.

She looked at him a little wildly. 'You mustn't,' she begged him. 'You should keep them on until tomorrow—that's twice in ten minutes.'

'So it is. I think all the excitement must have gone

to my head, don't you? So you must allow me a little license.'

He swooped suddenly and she was caught in an arm which pulled her close, and kissed. The kiss was thorough, and if anything had been needed to confirm her feelings for him, it would have done so a hundred times over.

He loosed her as suddenly as he had held her. 'A little relish for the ogre,' he observed, and opened the door. She went through it without looking at him; he wouldn't have had much opportunity to kiss girls while he had been on his enforced holiday, so it was natural that he should rectify the omission, and possibly he was regretting the brevity of his visitors' stay. But that had been his own fault. She hurried upstairs, not sure where she was going, but it really didn't matter as long as she could get away from him and the penetrating look from those grey eyes.

When she went down for tea an hour later, Benedict told her, 'Van Tromp is coming for dinner, and I should be glad of half an hour of your time, Cassandra—just before dinner, I think. Shall we say the library at half past six? Wear something pretty, you'll be off duty by then.'

She wore the blue patterned dress and for the first time was sorry she hadn't brought something more suitable for the evening with her. Mijnheer van Tromp was there as well as Benedict. They had been deep in conversation as she entered—about her, she felt sure, a feeling justified when Benedict said, 'Hullo—we're talking about you.'

She advanced into the room, confident that her calm manner quite disguised all her other feelings. 'I thought so,' she remarked pleasantly. 'One can always tell. What did you wish to see me about?'

He answered with no hesitation. 'You realize, of course, that I shall be returning to work in some form or other in a few days. Sooner than I had expected, as it happens, for I have just heard from Viske that everything is entirely satisfactory. It only remains for a general check-up tomorrow.'

She was a little impatient. Did he really suppose that she didn't know she was about to be given the sack? She said tartly, 'I quite understand. When do you wish me to leave?'

He contrived to look hurt. 'Cassandra Darling,' he said patiently, 'as usual you have leapt ahead and rushed over your bridge before you came to it. I was going to make you a rather nice speech of thanks. As it is, and since you want it that way—yes, dear girl, I am giving you the sack, for the very good reason—' his voice had become silky again, 'that even if you wore a uniform round the clock, once I have discarded my dark glasses, no one is going to believe that I need a nurse.'

He smiled at her, a mocking little smile which had the effect of increasing her ill humour out of all bounds.

'Well,' she uttered, 'you really are—of all the—I can't find words…'

'Good,' he sounded brisk, 'that will give me a chance to talk.'

'I don't want to hear any more. I'm very glad that you are quite recovered and will be able to work again, I'm quite ready to…'

'Perhaps if I might interrupt your interesting little discussion?' suggested Mijnheer van Tromp soothingly. 'There is something I wish you would do for me, Cassandra. My surgery nurse—she leaves tomorrow. I have another one coming, of course, but not for a little while. I was wondering if you would consider—as you are already here—filling the vacancy until she could take over? Your lack of Dutch will make very little difference, I fancy—my secretary answers the telephone for a good part of the day; you would have merely to admit my patients, give injections, find notes and so forth—quite simple.' He looked at her hopefully. 'I should be glad to pay you the same fee as you receive from Benedict.'

Cassandra could think of nothing at all to say; the sheer unexpectedness of it had taken her breath and woollied her wits; she wasn't even conscious of thinking sensibly about it. She asked at last, 'Should I really be of use?'

'I should be eternally grateful,' stated Mijnheer van Tromp.

'Well then, I'll be glad to help out for a little while.' She wasn't sure if she had meant to say that, but now it was said and she smiled at him, missing the look of triumphant satisfaction upon Benedict's face, 'When would you want me to start?'

'The day after tomorrow. My nurse will be there in the morning and will show you what there is to be done.'

'So you will have a day off tomorrow, Cassandra,' said Benedict.

'But I haven't worked long enough.'

'Let us not argue about that,' and this time his voice was remote and commanding. 'I suppose Cassandra will take over Lulu's room?'

'Lulu?' she was surprised into saying, 'What a funny name—for a nurse I mean.'

'Her own name is even funnier. No girl likes to be called Harmonia.'

Cassandra choked back a laugh and Mijnheer van Tromp explained:

'Lulu has a room just across the street from my house. It is a very pleasant room and I think you will be quite comfortable there. Shall Mevrouw Schat expect you tomorrow evening?'

'Very well—I'll come after tea.'

'Dinner,' interposed Benedict quietly. 'Don't forget that we are having a small gathering of friends tomorrow evening, Cor. Afterwards will do, I take it?'

He turned his face to Cassandra and said mildly, 'And before you speak out of turn, Cassandra, we shall be delighted to have your company tomorrow evening. Tante Beatrix will be desolated if you refuse.'

Hypnotized by the dark glasses, she found herself accepting meekly; she would have to have dinner somewhere, and she supposed the green would do—she really needed another dress. 'It won't be a big party?' she asked anxiously.

'If you are thinking about clothes and suchlike nonsense, there is no need. Anything will do.'

She loved him with all her heart, but how annoying a man could be! She was on the point of contradicting him flatly when Mijnheer van Tromp said quickly, 'I'm sure you will look very nice, Cassandra. Then I can rest assured that you will stay until my new nurse comes?' He had turned his back on his partner.

'Yes—about how long do you think that will be?'

He looked suddenly vague. 'Oh, a week—ten days. You will be home for Christmas.'

The prospect gave her no pleasure. How would her dear ogre spend Christmas, she wondered, and how many more pretty girls did he number amongst his acquaintances? She gave him a swift glance; his face was turned towards her, he might not be able to see her clearly, all the same she assumed a pleased expression. 'That will be delightful,' she told them.

'Then that's settled,' he had looked away from her and now he walked towards the door, his stick sweeping an invisible path before him. 'Shall we go and have a drink with Tante Beatrix?'

The evening passed off very well; Cassandra kept as far away from Benedict as she could, occupying herself exclusively with the old lady and when he showed signs of breaking into their conversation, she transferred her attention to his partner. At the end of the evening she was able to congratulate herself on her strategy, for they had exchanged barely a dozen words or so. At last she slipped quietly from the room and started up the stairs, then gave a soundless shriek as Benedict came across the hall and caught her around the waist. He had his glasses off again and even though the light was dim, she felt called upon to point this out to him. Benedict said something in his own language which sounded blunt, to say the least of it. 'You have avoided me for the entire evening,' he pointed out, this time in English. 'Why?'

She stood still, wary of his arm. 'Indeed I have not,' she assured him mendaciously, and took a tentative step backwards.

'When you tell fibs the tip of your nose quivers.' He was laughing at her. He was still laughing as he bent his head to kiss her with such gentleness that she felt tears in her eyes. When he let her go she hurried up the stairs, to pause when he called after her, 'You'll come with me tomorrow, you aren't being fired until the evening—and don't wear uniform, Cassandra!'

They were at the hospital in Utrecht by nine o'clock the following morning, and this time she stayed with Jan in the car. She watched Benedict, who had been met at the entrance by Mijnheer Viske, walk briskly away. Her eyes were glued on his disappearing back when Jan said, 'Half an hour for the check-up, Miss Cassandra, and another half an hour for a final look at his eyes, do you not think? And then he must try his new spectacles, and of course they will talk. You are happy to sit here, or you wish for a little drive?'

She said quickly, 'Let's stay here, Jan, just in case…' she left the thought unspoken, but he understood, for he said at once:

'Don't worry, he will be all right. To pass the time I will tell you about my daughter and my wife, that is if you would like to hear—it is not altogether nice, the story…perhaps you would rather not know, after all?'

'But I would—you don't mind? It won't be too painful for you to remember?'

His laugh was bitter. 'The pain remains, deep inside me, and I remember for always. If it had not been for Mijnheer, I should have gone mad.'

Cassandra turned a little in her seat. 'Tell me,' she urged him.

'I met Mijnheer van Manfeld in this hospital. I had lost my memory, you see, I did not know who I was—to this day I do not know. They took me off the streets and because I had something very wrong with my throat he came to see me. He saw these too,' he touched the sleeve of his coat lightly, 'and he guessed, and because I could not understand his language, he tried others—French, English, German, and when he spoke German I became enraged and spoke my own tongue, and as good fortune would have it, he understood a little of what I said, for he has a small knowledge of Polish. He took me to his home as soon as I was well, and asked me no questions but let me work—in the garden, round the house and then driving the car. And slowly there were things I remembered, terrible things, and he shared them with me; he made me see reason again; he dragged me back to life and even contentment. He was a young man then, for it was twelve years ago—barely twenty-four and a registrar at this hospital where he is now a senior consultant.'

'But the war had been over for fifteen years when he found you…'

'There were some who were lost or forgotten or who, like myself, wandered through Europe looking for their wives and children, their parents—anyone who belonged to them.'

She put a hand on his arm. 'Jan, how terrible, and I'm so very sorry, but I'm glad too that Mijnheer van Manfeld found you. No wonder you are such good friends. Don't you remember what you did before…?'

'No. I was, I think, adequately educated, but you see I don't know my name—I am not sure of my age, but I believe that I am about sixty, perhaps older. I do not remember what part of Poland I came from, Mijnheer has taken me back there to try and discover—but it was impossible; I can remember nothing of it.'

'But you remember that you have—had a wife and daughter.'

He looked straight ahead of him, his hands clenched on the wheel. 'Yes, they took us away, but not together. My wife and daughter one way and I another. They laughed about it.'

Cassandra wanted to cry. 'There's no chance?' she began gently.

He smiled at her. 'No—only if there should be a miracle. You see, Mijnheer has done everything—he has spent time and much effort and a great deal of money—he is a good man, Miss Cassandra.'

They were still talking quietly when Benedict came out of the hospital, accompanied by Mijnheer Viske and the radiologist. He wasn't wearing the dark glasses any more, but tinted ones. They made him look different, and if possible, even more handsome. He paused at the entrance just long enough to say good-bye and then came quickly to the car.

'Move over, Jan,' he said quietly, 'I'm driving.'

Cassandra, without being asked, got out and got in the back and sat silent while he drove back the way he had come, along the motorway, and very fast. Beyond a brief, smiling nod, he hadn't spoken to her, but he and Jan talked, and in their own language, so that she was unable to understand a word, but they seemed pleased with themselves and when he said over one shoulder, 'Well, Cassandra, what do you think of my new glasses?' she said brightly, 'Oh, super—how wonderful you must feel.'

He nodded, his eyes on the road, and didn't speak to her again until he drew up outside the house.

'Get in the front,' he ordered, 'we're going to have the rest of the day off.' He grinned at Jan, who didn't seem in the least surprised but waved and smiled and went indoors as Benedict turned the car and took it back through Rhenen's main street again. They were going towards Utrecht once more, but on the edge of the town he took a narrow road on the left which wound uphill—the first hill she remembered being on since she had arrived in Holland. There were a few houses to begin with, then nothing but trees and shrubs until they came abruptly on to its flattened top. There was a tall square tower with a pointed turret there, and around it and built into it, a hotel.

'We're going to have lunch here,' said Benedict, 'but first we'll go for a walk—there's a splendid view.'

She got out obediently and he took her arm and walked her past the hotel on to a narrow path between the trees of the wood which crowned the hill's top. They thinned presently to allow them to see the Rhine beyond and below them, and still further away, the Waal, very clear in the sharp winter morning. 'It's lonely here,' he remarked. 'We haven't been alone—really alone, since we came back to Rhenen.'

She shot him a puzzled look. 'I hadn't noticed that you wanted to be, and we went for that drive.'

'Yes,' his mouth curved in a smile but he didn't pursue the subject which she found a pity, instead he asked, 'You like the idea of working for van Tromp?'

'Yes, very much. I hope I shan't get into too many difficulties with the language, though.'

They had come to a dried-up stream, not very wide. He strode over, lifted her after him and said, 'Well, you'll have to make a start somewhere,' and kissed her, such a light kiss that it would have been foolish to have taken account of it. He took her arm again and walked her briskly up the hill, with the little wood on one side of them, and fields sloping away on the other.

'It's nice here,' said Cassandra, 'of course that's why you came, to see the view.'

She wasn't looking at him, so she didn't see him smile and all he said was, 'We'll have lunch, shall we?'

The hotel was nice; comfortable, almost luxurious, with wide views from its windows overlooking the river. The meal was delicious, and it was after two o'clock when at last they got up to go. The afternoon was already dimming into an early dusk as they went out to the car. All the same, Benedict said: 'A short run, don't you think?'

And Cassandra, happy and uncaring of the future, agreed eagerly.

Back home at Rhenen, she paused in the hall to

thank him for her day. 'It was lovely, and I hadn't expected it,' she laughed up at him.

He went with her to the foot of the staircase. 'No?' He kissed her lightly and said on a laugh, 'I'm beginning to make a habit of that, aren't I?'

She answered him seriously. 'No, it seems to me to be quite a natural thing to do after living a monk's life for weeks.'

He was still laughing. 'Is that what you imagine my *raison d'être* is? To kiss girls?'

She laughed. 'I don't think that at all,' she assured him, and fell silent. Then she said, 'I don't know anything about you—have you a family?'

His eyes were bright behind the glasses. 'No—my parents are dead and I have no brothers or sisters—no family.' His face became bland. 'Are you going to urge me to marry and create a family for myself?'

'It isn't my business to urge you to do anything,' she pointed out huffily, 'and even if I wanted to, I wouldn't, because,' she went on a little obscurely, 'if I did you would call me Miss Busybody.' She paused. 'Aren't you lonely?'

She had asked the question seriously, but his tone was light. 'If I remember my story books, ogres are lonely.'

She corrected him earnestly. 'Oh, no, not all of them. The one on top of the beanstalk had a wife—only she was afraid of him.'

'And have you ever been afraid of anyone, Cassandra?'

She considered carefully. 'I don't think so.'

'And you're not afraid of me?'

She was quite taken aback. 'Heavens, no. Why?'

'Perhaps you pitied me too much?'

'No. At least, perhaps at first when the children told me about you and when I was in the shop and Jan bought almost no groceries and I thought perhaps you were very poor. That must seem very silly to you, with your great hampers of food—that's why I made a cake. You weren't very nice when I called.'

'No. You see I thought you had come out of idle curiosity. It wasn't until you bounced off, quivering with temper that I knew how very wrong I had been. Jan was very annoyed with me, you see, he fell under your spell the moment he set eyes on you.'

Her voice was sharp. 'I don't know how to weave spells. I'd better go and pack.'

He had turned away, saying carelessly, 'Ah, yes, of course. You're leaving this evening, aren't you?'

She was almost at the top of the stairs when he called after her,

'Wear that green dress, you look pretty in it.'

When she went downstairs later the room was full of people, or so it seemed to her as she went in, and some of them, she saw with relief, she had already met. Benedict, standing by the window talking to a burly man and a striking-looking girl, put down his glass and came across the room to meet her before walking her round, introducing her to those she didn't know and waiting beside her while she exchanged greetings with those she did. They ended up by the couple he had been talking to; the man he introduced as Doctor van der Pol and the girl as his sister Paula, who, on closer inspection, proved to be older than Cassandra had first thought, but undeniably attractive. She was beautifully turned out too and, worst of all, on the friendliest terms with Benedict, far closer terms than those of his other two visitors, for as they talked she put a hand on his arm and almost at once he covered it with his own with a brief gesture. Cassandra looked away and then looked quickly at his face to find him looking at her, a very faint smile curving his lips, so that she went a bright pink, giving him the hateful opportunity to ask her if she found the room too warm.

'No,' she said coldly, and turned away.

The dinner was a leisurely one, and it was only when Tante Beatrix had led the ladies from the room, because she was old-fashioned enough to consider that the men should be left to themselves for a little while, that Cassandra saw that it was almost ten o'clock.

'You look anxious,' said Paula beside her. 'Are you tired, perhaps?'

Cassandra explained that she was to leave that evening and Paula said pleasantly, 'Oh, yes, Benedict told me. I shouldn't worry, arrangements will have been made.' She looked over her shoulder as she spoke and went on, 'Here they are—Benedict, here is Cassandra very worried because she feels that she is forgotten. You will reassure her?'

'Of course,' he was smiling. 'Van Tromp will leave in about half an hour, Cassandra, and will take you with him. You're ready, I expect?' He went on in careless apology, 'I should have told you sooner, shouldn't I?' He turned to Paula. 'We have been talking about Christmas—we shall be far apart, all of us—you in Scotland, Cassandra, and Paula in Canada, and van Tromp in France, even Teake will be away…'

'And you?' Cassandra asked because she simply had to know.

He allowed his glance to drop momentarily to her face. 'I? Not here.'

She bade her quiet good-byes after that and went and fetched her things, then said good-bye to Jan and Miep. She had only been in the house a few days, and yet she felt sad at leaving it and sadder still because she was leaving Benedict.

She found him in the hall with his partner. 'Ready?' he asked her, far too cheerfully. 'No need to say good-bye, I'm sure to see you. Good luck with the job.'

She put out a hand because everyone shook hands, didn't they? At least she had learnt that. He took it and said seriously, 'Thank you, Cassandra, for everything,' and went to open the door. She followed Mijnheer van Tromp through it, out to his big Citroen car, got in beside him, and didn't look back.

CHAPTER SEVEN

THE journey was so short it seemed hardly worth while to have got into the car. Cassandra, her mind still full of Benedict, found herself getting out almost immediately and following Mijnheer van Tromp through the door of a little gabled house in a row of similar houses.

'Mevrouw Schat will be in the kitchen,' he told her. 'She will take you to your room, and tomorrow at half past seven she will give you your breakfast and then come across the street to my house—number seventeen—my name is on the door. Lulu will be there and will show you everything. You will work with her until midday, so that you can learn the—the…'

'Ropes,' supplied Cassandra. 'I'll be there. Thank you for bringing me and arranging everything, I hope Mevrouw Schat…'

The lady bearing that name joined them at that moment. The hall was small and narrow; she was a large woman, not fat, but strongly built and tall, so that the hall seemed even smaller than it was. They all went into the kitchen, a small, very neat place, not in the least modern but cosy, with a great many pot plants on shelves and bright gingham curtains.

Mevrouw Schat, having shaken hands with great vigour, broke into voluble talk. She went on for some time and when she paused for breath Cassandra said, 'I'm not sure if this is going to work, Mijnheer van Tromp. I have no idea what she's saying.'

He smiled at her in a kindly fashion. 'She says nothing important, only that Lulu left her room today and she hopes that you will be comfortable while you are here, and that you will come downstairs for your breakfast at half past seven exactly. Would you like me to stay for a little while, or will you be all right?'

She wasn't sure about that, but she would have to make a start some time and it might as well be now. 'I'll be fine,' she assured him, 'I'll be at your house in the morning, and thank you for bringing me.'

They wished each other good night and Cassandra went up to her room, unpacked, wrote a brief letter to Rachel and went to bed. But not to sleep; the party would still be in full swing at Benedict's house; that girl Paula would have him all to herself. Cassandra wondered about her; if they were such close friends why hadn't she been to see him sooner, and why hadn't he mentioned her?—although, she told herself severely, there was absolutely no reason why he should have done. He had taken her out, been charming to her, but then, she supposed, any man would have done the same. Kissing, she told herself uneasily, meant nothing at all, and where would he be at Christmas? In Canada with Paula? She was beginning to get a headache; she forced her thoughts into other channels—presents to take home, the clothes she would buy when she got back to England, the job she would get, and always at the back of her mind there was the thought of Benedict to make nonsense of her efforts.

She was punctual for her breakfast, and as soon as she had finished she crossed the street to the doctor's house where she found Lulu waiting for her.

Lulu was middle-sized and plump, with a cheerful, pretty face and bright blue eyes. Moreover, she spoke English of a sort.

The work was a good deal easier than she had anticipated. Unlike hospital, there was no rush and hurry; she had time enough to puzzle over the names, file away the used cards and get out new ones as they were wanted. She even managed the telephone. Mijnheer van Tromp had put his head round the door to wish her good luck and them both a good morning, and by lunch time she felt fairly confident that given a few days at this pace, she would be able to cope quite nicely, and after all, it wasn't for long. She had chaperoned one or two of the patients too, in the well-equipped alcove in the consulting room, and that had been easy too; the instruments were the same, the method of examination was the same, and anything she needed to know, either Lulu or Mijnheer van Tromp told her. When she and Lulu said good-bye she felt almost at home, and reasonably sure of herself.

It was almost half past three when Mijnheer van

Tromp called her on the intercom and asked her to go to his consulting room. There was no patient there, and none due for the next twenty minutes. Cassandra crossed the waiting room, tapped on his door and went in. He was standing at the window, Benedict beside him, and on the desk was a tea-tray.

Both men turned to look at her as she went in and the elder said:

'My dear, will you pour the tea? I usually contrive to have a cup about this time and here is Benedict to share it with us. There is one more patient, I believe? Then I have some visits; if you would stay here until my return, to take any calls and clear up and so forth. I will leave the addresses of the patients I shall be visiting.'

She said, 'Very well, sir,' wished Benedict a brief good afternoon and went to the tea-tray to pour out. There were three cups, and she was still pouring the second when he said, 'Of course you will have a cup with us, Cassandra.'

She thanked him, handed them their cups and sat down composedly to drink her own tea. The two men would probably talk shop and it never entered her head to encourage them to do otherwise, but apparently they had other ideas, for her employer came to sit behind his desk and Benedict sat on the corner of the desk itself, looking so suave and elegant and unlike himself that she felt she didn't know him.

'A slice of your cake would be very nice now,' he

told her, and then when she didn't speak, 'We all miss you very much, Cassandra.'

She smiled then and he added: 'Did Lulu make everything clear?'

'Oh, yes, thank you. She's a dear.' She looked at Mijnheer van Tromp. 'You'll miss her dreadfully, won't you?'

'My loss is also my gain, my dear.' He gave her a gallant little bow. 'I can't think of anyone I would rather have in her place.'

She smiled widely, showing an unexpected dimple. 'How nicely you put it—I hope I can live up to that.'

Benedict came over to the desk, carrying his cup which she filled, milked and sugared in a stern, no-nonsense fashion, inquiring: 'Sweet enough?'

He stood looking down at her, smiling a little. 'Just right,' he told her affably. 'You must know by now that I don't like too much sweetness, and that applies to people too.'

She went a little red, for it seemed to her that he was making one of his nasty remarks which she could never answer; instead she asked:

'Are you enjoying your first day back to work?'

'Very much. Will you come and have dinner with us tomorrow evening?'

She refused to be ruffled by the sudden thumping of her heart. 'That would be nice—is it to be another party?'

'No—it may astonish you to know that I seldom give parties. You'll come?'

'Well—yes, thank you. About seven o'clock?'

'Earlier if you can manage to get away from this old despot.' He grinned at his partner, who chuckled and said: 'Now, now—I am mildness itself, am I not, Cassandra?'

She agreed with him nicely, rose to her feet, and murmuring something suitable about work to do, got herself out of the room.

She was kept busy for the rest of the afternoon, for even when there were no patients, there was the filing to see to and the cards to get ready for the morning as well as the consulting room to put to rights. She was to be free the following day after one o'clock, too; Mijnheer van Tromp went to a nursing home in the afternoon and there were no patients at his house; she would have to think of something to do; go to Utrecht or Arnhem perhaps, and look at the shops, and a nice long walk on Sunday.

It was colder than ever the next morning and during the night it had snowed quite hard so that everything was white, excepting the sky, which was a dull and uniform grey. During breakfast Mevrouw Schat managed to make her understand that there was ice on the river and that the weather would probably get worse, but Cassandra, thinking of the evening ahead, couldn't have cared less. She draped herself in the cape, crossed the street and became at once immersed in her work.

There weren't many patients that morning, and excepting for a little confusion on the telephone because the secretary hadn't come, she was managing very well. The first patient had been in for some few minutes when Mijnheer van Tromp threw open his door and crossed the waiting room with a haste which brought her to her feet and half way to meet him.

He wasted no words. 'Get your cloak and go down to the street. Benedict will be there with the car. Go with him—there has been an accident.'

She nodded, snatched at her cloak and flew outside. It had begun to snow again, but she had no time to draw more than one icy breath before the Aston Martin slid to a halt before her and the door was opened. 'Good girl!' said Benedict. 'Get in.'

The snow was quite deep. Cassandra squelched the yard or so, the cloak dragging wetly about her, and got in. He hardly gave her time to shut the door, but was off again, driving fast down the narrow street towards the river.

'A dredger and a barge,' he told her with a calm she envied. 'Some of the dredger's machinery broke away and caught the barge as it was passing—they're drifting in mid-river, locked together. I gather that there are several injured—the fire people and the police are already on the way.' He shot round a corner and gave her a sideways glance. 'Get that Wagnerian garment off, dear girl, or you'll be overboard and sunk without trace before we get there—and that fetching cap. There's an old sweater of mine in the back—put it on.'

She did as she had been bidden, noticing for the first time that he was wearing a thick sweater himself. She had managed to get the cloak off, her cap as well, and was pulling on the sweater when he came to a skidding halt by a small jetty, surrounded by small houses, packed together, tumbling almost to the water's edge. There were several people there. Cassandra thrust her head through the sweater's neck with disastrous results to her hair, pushed the sleeves up her arms, and jumped out of the car.

There was a small boat with a man at the tiller waiting for them. She eyed it with some apprehension; possibly, if she had been given time, she might have voiced her doubts about it, but Benedict's hand was firm under her elbow, she was sitting in it before she had had the time to so much as open her mouth. He draped an extremely smelly oilskin round her shoulders, said cheerfully, 'We shan't be long now,' and sat down beside her with no concern whatever for the alarming rocking of the boat.

He had his bag with him, held firm between his feet, and turned his head to say, 'I didn't have much time to think, I added a few things I thought we might need—there's a man with a lacerated throat, that I do know, but what else…' He shrugged his shoulders and put a quiet hand over hers. 'Nice having you,' he said, and then, 'Here, I'll plait that hair—whatever happened to it?'

'I had to put on your sweater,' she reminded him, 'in a confined space and without a mirror.'

His laugh was enough to rock the boat. 'Poor Cassandra, but it won't matter what you look like, you know.'

She answered soberly. 'No, I know that.' Had it ever mattered what she looked like to him? she wondered as she looked round her. They were well away from the shore now, nearing the hopelessly tangled mass swinging slowly to and fro in the water, and Mevrouw Schat had been right, there was ice on the river. She stared at it, wondering why she didn't feel cold. 'How many men on board do you expect?' she asked.

'Not many, thank heaven. It's a Rhine barge. The owner and his family will be on board, I suppose, there are maybe half a dozen on the dredger. By the time we've done first aid and got them ashore the medical team and the ambulances should be here though the snow will slow them down.'

The little boat danced uneasily round the ruins of the barge, looking for a place where they could get aboard, then someone called from the tangle of ironwork on the dredger and the boatman crept in close and before Cassandra could tell Benedict that nothing on earth would make her climb on to the slippery, heaving deck before her, several hands shot out, and with a useful shove from behind, she found herself aboard.

Benedict had joined her before she had time to do

more than cast a fearful glance around her. The men—firemen, she thought they were—spoke urgently to him and he caught her by the arm, saying 'This way,' and helped her through the twisted steel. They had already freed two of the crew; one was conscious with a bruised swelling over one eye, the other had a jagged tear in his throat and was in a poor way. Benedict was already on his knees, opening his case. 'Tracheotomy,' he said briefly. 'The stuff's in the white linen roll—open it, dear girl, and do your stuff.'

It went very well, considering they had to work under almost impossible conditions, with the dredger heaving up and down beneath them and nothing really sterile. But there was a great deal of willing help; Cassandra handed Benedict the knife because there wasn't any time to lose, the tube to be inserted and left for her to tie with its tapes, the swabs, a paper towel upon which to clean his hands... When Benedict was sure that the man was out of immediate danger, she asked, 'Do you want me to stay with him?'

He was on his feet again. 'No—here's someone who'll stay.' He spoke briefly to a burly policeman, said, rather unfairly, 'Come along, girl, there's no time for you to moon about,' and pushed and pulled her over another heap of wreckage.

The man they found lying on the other side was held fast by a leg, hopelessly caught in a tangle of splintered wood, wire ropes and heavy iron chains.

It wasn't so much the weight of the stuff, she thought, it was the diabolical manner in which the leg had been caught up and twisted and torn until it was no longer a leg. The man was unconscious. Benedict took a look, felt for the man's pulse, said briefly, 'Off, I'm afraid. Thank God he's unconscious. I'll give him an intravenous—there's some pentothal—good girl! I'll have to do a guillotine below thigh—forceps in that plated tin, that's right—ligatures in the flap, scissors at the bottom somewhere, you'll have to cut as I tie—we'll want someone to take—ah, good man!' He was speaking Dutch now and Cassandra wondered at his coolness. Two firemen with a stretcher had stationed themselves close by. She shut her mind to everything but the job before them to such good effect that when the swift operation was over, the patient on the stretcher borne away towards a waiting boat and the mess cleared up, Benedict said quietly, 'What a splendid nurse you are, Cassandra. I couldn't have managed without you.'

She blushed and said hastily, 'Thank you—don't you want me to go with that man?'

'No—come,' and she stumbled after him, across the dredger's deck to its side where it was hopelessly entangled with the barge, and when he stepped from one heaving deck to the other and turned to give her a hand, she scrambled over too, her mind boggling at the things she was doing—the most unlikely and awful things, enough to make her stand in the middle of the deck and burst into tears, but it was obvious that Benedict didn't expect her to do anything so silly; she flung her untidy plait over her shoulder, and, her hand in his, made her way with him to the wheelhouse of the barge. There was someone there— a child. She could see a small arm, warmly clad in a gay anorak, hanging through its broken window.

'Hurry!' she cried to Benedict. 'Perhaps he's all right, we must get him out,' but he had pushed ahead of her and was standing deliberately between her and the child.

Presently he turned round. 'There's no need for us here,' he said harshly, and when she protested: 'But are you sure? Shouldn't we at least try?' he told her quite roughly, 'No, Cassandra, it's useless,' and pulled her back the way they had come towards a group of men standing round two of the crew.

One was a head injury and unconscious. Benedict ordered him ashore as quickly as maybe, and turned to the second man.

The last case had gone at last, and she was standing, wet and filthy and bloodstained, her hair whipped in a tangle by an icy wind, listening to the faraway sound of the ambulance klaxons on the shore, when she became aware that she was feeling sick. When Benedict, his bag closed at last, said, 'Come along, girl—home,' she faltered, 'I'm so sorry, I can't—I feel awful.'

It was mortifying and doubly so because he laughed at her, but even as he laughed he was doing all the right things. Exhausted and whiter than skimmed milk, she sat on the deck, Benedict's arm round her shoulders. She felt better now, only so very cold; even the vast thick sweater she was wearing seemed like tissue paper. She shivered and he said at once:

'Home, and a change of clothes and a hot bath. Come along.'

This time he lifted her from one deck to the other and didn't put her down again, but passed her to the boatman's waiting arms before he joined them in the boat. The water was still heaving nastily, but the queasiness had gone, she was even able to wave to the policemen left on board to clear up the mess preparatory to moving the vessels out of the river traffic's way. She was lifted out of the boat on to dry land too, draped in a filthy blanket and wondering if she looked as dreadful as she smelled, but at least she felt warmer now and Benedict's arms were strong and comforting and she had no doubt that he looked just as awful. He dumped her in the car, got in beside her, and drove straight to his own house, and when she protested that she should go to Mevrouw Schat's, he said 'Rubbish,' in a reassuring voice, and carried her into the house.

In the fragrant hot bath ten minutes later, Cassandra was surprised to find herself in tears, she wasn't sure why—excitement, nerves stretched too far, the memory of the child in the wheelhouse, all the nasty jobs she had been called upon to do. She had the good sense to have a good cry while she was about it, then tidied up her face and feeling much better, went back into the bedroom, to stand still, struck by the thought that she had no clothes. But someone else had thought of that too, for on the bed, side by side, lay a long-sleeved, high-necked nightie, and a quilted dressing gown ruffled at the neck and wrists and of a delicate pink. Cassandra put them on and was nearly downstairs when Benedict, back in his clerical grey, came out of the library.

'In here,' he invited, and held the door open for her and then shut it behind him and stood against it, inspecting her. 'Delightful,' he observed. 'Now we'll have lunch, shall we, then Jan shall fetch you some clothes and you can do whatever you had planned to do this afternoon, but remember I'm coming for you this evening—about six.'

She remembered now that she had planned to buy the new dress and her consternation showed on her face so that he said quite sharply, 'Something's not right—what's the matter?'

She found herself telling him, because he wasn't the remote surgeon he had become within the last few days, but her ogre. When she had finished he smiled at her with kindness. 'Well, that's soon settled. I'll take you there after lunch and you can buy the dress, only I've a couple of calls to make, so you'll have to wait in the car. You won't mind?'

'No—oh no. It's very kind of you.'

He laughed at that and pulled her to her feet and

instead of letting her go, put his arms around her and she stood quietly, wanting it to last for ever. When he kissed her, she returned his kiss, careless for once of showing her feelings.

He let her go, staring down into her face, unsmiling so that, suddenly troubled, she said in a little rush, 'You mustn't—we—I'd forgotten Paula...'

He smiled then, his eyes gleaming with amusement. 'So had I. Were we supposed to remember her for any special reason?'

She drew back a little and he let her go, and somehow the gesture annoyed her. 'Well,' she began, 'you and Paula...' She tried again: 'Oh, well, I mean I know it's not important to you, but she might not like...'

'Is it important to you?' He looked interested and still amused.

'That has nothing to do with it. It's—it's...'

He became truly the ogre again. 'And Miss Busybody has been hard at it again, arranging people's lives to her own satisfaction—is it to your satisfaction, Cassandra?' He smiled thinly. 'Have you married me off to Paula, is that it, on the strength of seeing us together once? I've a very good mind to oblige you.' His voice became a subdued roar. 'God's teeth, can you not mind your own business, worming your way into my life with homemade cakes and hoity-toity airs; twiddling Jan round your little finger! Even Miep cries because you have left us.'

'I've told you before, you're not to say that,' Cassandra reproved him coldly. 'And why, suddenly, are you in such a nasty temper? You've no reason at all—you had some excuse while you were living on Mull, but now everything is fine again.' Her voice became a little shrill. 'And I have never wormed my way into your life! I made you a cake because I th-thought you were l-lonely and p-poor. How was I to know that you're awash with money and fabulous houses and hordes of people to look after you?'

'There you go, exaggerating again! I am well-to-do, but no millionaire, and though I grant you I have a lovely home, I feel that I should point out to you that save for a very small cottage in the south of France, it is the only home I have, and I have yet to see hordes of servants in it.'

'Don't quibble!' she urged him snappishly. 'You know exactly what I mean. You're being very—very…'

She was plucked off her feet and engulfed in his arms once more.

'I agree entirely, and I have no right to tease you, my poor girl. You shall eat your lunch and I'll take you back to get some clothes, then we can go and buy that dress which I feel sure will turn you into a beautiful princess.'

He kissed her, but this time gently, as he would have kissed a child and she forbore from telling him that there was no dress on earth which could transform her from her ordinary self. Instead, with his arm around her shoulders, she went meekly to her lunch.

They were met at Mevrouw Schat's front door by that good lady herself, voluble in her sympathy, clucking like a nice motherly hen. Fifteen minutes later, Cassandra was dressed and following him out to the car. It was snowing again and getting dark, and the brightly lighted shops looked inviting.

'Which one?' asked Benedict, tooling down the main street, and when she pointed it out to him, slid the car to a careful stop. 'How long?' he wanted to know.

'I don't know, but please don't wait. You've got your visits, I can perfectly well...'

'Don't twitter. I've a visit close by, then I shall come back here. Don't hurry, I'll wait.' He smiled at her and drove away and she went into the shop.

A quarter of an hour later, she was outside again, light of heart as well as pocket, for the dress was a perfect fit and even in her own hypercritical eyes it did something for her. She stood quite happily waiting for him in the cold, savouring the pleasurable fact that she would wear it that evening, a little excited too. He came a few moments later, slipping out of a side street into the stream of traffic with neat precision. She got in when he opened the door and deposited the box carefully on the back seat.

'Found something you like?' he asked carelessly, his mind so obviously on something else that she made her answer brief. 'Yes, thank you,' was all she said, stifling disappointment, but it was something more than disappointment when he continued. 'Sorry you had to wait. I didn't think you would be ready— women never are when they go shopping—but I met Paula.'

He had taken the car out of the town by now, on to the Wageringen Road and the traffic had thinned. Cassandra managed a pleasant: 'Oh, yes? I shall see her this evening, I expect,' and hoped that he would say no.

'She couldn't manage dinner, and I'm hoping you and Tante Beatrix won't think me too ill-mannered if I go out about nine o'clock—it may have to be earlier.' He threw her a quick glance. 'I wouldn't suggest it to anyone else, but this is something which matters.'

She had no idea how she managed to keep her voice so sweetly reasonable. 'I'm sure neither your aunt nor I will mind in the very least. But why have dinner with us at all if it's so important?'

Incredibly he answered, 'Well, of course that would help enormously; I didn't dare to suggest it, though—you're sure you don't mind? I shall be back all the sooner—in time to walk you back to Mevrouw Schat.'

'Now that would be silly,' she told him, nothing in her voice betraying the cold rage inside her. 'It's barely two minutes' walk, and if I need an escort surely I can ask Jan.'

He was silent for so long she thought he might not

have heard. When he did speak his voice was pleased. 'What a nice girl you are, Cassandra! Most women would be quite put out. But perhaps we know each other too well for that?'

She agreed mildly although it would have been nice to have exploded. This, she told herself, was what came of being plain and sensible; this was what she could expect for climbing on and off heaving decks in a biting wind and when any other girl with a grain of sense would have refused point blank. And she had come running across Europe at his whim, hadn't she? She was a fool.

After his visits Benedict drove her straight to Mevrouw Schat's little house. As he went away, he called, 'Don't be late this evening!'

Against her better judgment Cassandra put on the new dress, although she could see little point in doing so. She ate a delicious dinner in Tante Beatrix's company and afterwards sat in the sitting-room, playing Scrabble with the old lady, who had a passion for the game. But as soon as she decently could, she made her excuses, pleading a fancied cold.

'And no wonder,' commented Mevrouw van Manfeld tartly, 'dragging you off to that terrible accident, just as though you were some boy. Benedict should be ashamed of himself!'

'Oh, no, you mustn't say that,' begged Cassandra, quite put out. 'I'm a nurse, you know, and that's how he thinks of me. Nurses go wherever they're wanted.'

Tante Beatrix uttered a sound which sounded like

Bah! and as Cassandra got up to fetch her coat, went on warmly: 'It's time he thought of you as a girl.'

Cassandra thought of the way he had kissed her; had he thought of her as a girl then or had she merely been there, a stand-in for the real thing? She thought she would never know. She went to the kitchen, said good night to Miep and Jan, and refusing Jan's offer to see her home, wished Tante Beatrix a good night too and started off down the street. She had made up her mind that she would be gone by the time Benedict got home and she had no intention of delaying any longer. She was turning the corner when she heard a car at the far end. It wasn't easy to run on the icy pavement, but she did. She was indoors, saying a rather breathless good night to Mevrouw Schat and racing up to her room, within minutes.

She was tearing off her clothes at a fine speed when her landlady called up the stairs. Cassandra ignored her and took the pins out of her hair; she was fairly sure that it was Benedict downstairs, come to apologize again, she muttered angrily. Well, she was almost in bed, wasn't she? Nothing would get her downstairs again until the morning. She wrapped her dressing-gown around her with a gesture worthy of grand opera and washed her face at the funny little basin in the corner of the room. She was brushing her teeth when there was a thunderous knock on the door. From her sparse knowledge of the Dutch language she dredged up two words which were identical in both languages and summed up the situation to a nicety. 'In bed!' she called, and went on with her toothbrushing.

The door was flung open. 'I said you were a liar,' said Benedict blandly from the door, 'and what are you hiding behind that toothbrush for? Afraid I'm going to snarl at you for not waiting for me? You're right, I am. What possessed you to come back so early? I told you I would return—and what's all this nonsense about a cold? Great healthy girls like you don't catch cold.'

'I am not a great healthy girl!' she said furiously. 'You make me sound like jolly hockey sticks or something—and get out of my room!'

Her speech didn't have the desired effect; he came in and shut the door after him.

'Mevrouw Schat,' she hissed at him, 'whatever will she think? She's old-fashioned—do go away!'

He raised innocent eyebrows. 'Go away? When I've only just come and Mevrouw Schat has gone to make coffee for us—we're going to drink it together in her front parlour; it's all very proper in her old-fashioned eyes too—I'm a doctor, remember? and you had a nasty experience this morning; you're still suffering from shock. I told her about that nasty cold you've invented too, so you can come downstairs in your dressing-gown with the greatest propriety.'

'I don't wish to come downstairs.' Cassandra still had the toothbrush in her hand and a faint moustache of toothpaste. She remembered where he had been and said with a kind of sadness, 'I didn't know you were like this,' she began, and then changed it to, 'There was no need for you to come here. I had a very pleasant evening, we played S-Scrabble.'

She turned her back on him and swallowed tears and toothpaste together and rinsed her brush elaborately. He was still there when she looked round; she couldn't make out the expression in his eyes because of the tinted glasses, and he was standing with his back to the light too.

He spoke impatiently. 'You are a silly girl. I thought women knew when a man was—er—interested.'

She shook her head. 'Here's one who doesn't.' She made her voice quiet and calm while her heart beat fit to crack her ribs.

He hadn't moved an inch, but his smile made the distance between them negligible. 'Well, start learning now, Cassandra—dear Cassandra.'

It was really too much. She said, near to tears, 'Oh, how can you talk like that? You were so different at the Relish—now I don't know what to think. You've come straight from Paula...'

'Hot foot,' he assured her blandly. He was leaning against the door, watching her; waiting for her to say something. She decided that she wouldn't, but her treacherous tongue disobeyed her. 'You asked me to go to dinner at your house and then you went out with—with...and you expect me to be glad to see you, and you couldn't be—be more...'

'Right?' he suggested helpfully. 'Now I'm the one

who's glad. But I mustn't be impatient, must I? I'll let your temper cool first. Come downstairs and I'll tell you about Paula.'

'No!'

'Afraid?' his voice was affable.

'Don't be ridiculous!' She had a stream of hair over one shoulder, twisting and untwisting it at a great rate.

'I'm prepared to carry you down,' Benedict offered mildly.

He meant it. She went past him through the door he held open for her and down the stairs into the parlour where Mevrouw Schat was polishing two silver spoons on her apron. She put them with a satisfied air into the saucers as they went in and when Benedict said something to her, looked in a motherly fashion at Cassandra, said '*Arme kind*', patted her shoulder kindly and went to fetch the coffee.

'What did she say?' asked Cassandra, momentarily diverted.

'Poor child,' he translated for her. 'You'll find a hot water bottle in your bed, I expect, and two eggs for breakfast.'

She couldn't stop the giggle. As she poured the coffee it struck her how strange it was that she and Benedict could quarrel and bicker and, five minutes later, laugh together. She handed him his coffee and sat down to drink her own.

'Now listen,' said Benedict. 'I've known Paula almost all my life, and I'm fond of her—friends become fond of each other, you know. She is engaged to one of my closest friends who is at present in Canada. When he went there a year ago he asked me to look after her, and I have done just that, in every way I could. So that when she wanted my help urgently concerning a house they are buying in Utrecht, I gave it. That the arrangements could only be made this evening was sheer misfortune for me. She is going to Canada to marry him very shortly, then they will come back here and settle down.' He paused and sighed and Cassandra asked quickly, 'Why are you sad about it?'

'Because I'm envious, I suppose.' He smiled and said quickly, 'I didn't get any dinner either.'

She was on her feet at once, the niggling doubt at the back of her mind she hadn't had time to examine forgotten. 'You must be famished. I'm sure Mevrouw Schat has something—soup, or sandwiches.' But he shook his head. 'Miep will have got something ready for me and I can't stay. One of my patients isn't too good, so I promised her husband I'd look in.'

He got to his feet. 'Good night, Cassandra. Wasn't she the daughter of the King of Troy, and could she not see into the future? Can you do that, I wonder?'

All at once he sounded tired. Cassandra said, quite gently, that she didn't think she could, wished him goodnight, and went up to bed. She lay awake a long time wondering why he had told her that he was envious. He had been rather horrid when she had taken it for granted that he was in love with Paula;

he probably was, she told herself miserably, but
Paula wanted the other man, his friend—and all poor
Benedict could do was fulfil the role of a faithful
friend to them both and hide his grief under ill-
temper and impatience. She thought she understood
him now, only it was a pity she didn't know how to
help him. On that thought she finally went to sleep.

CHAPTER EIGHT

MIJNHEER VAN TROMP was very kind the next morning; he asked Cassandra if she felt quite fit to work, commended her upon her courage, and wanted to know, with a look of great innocence, if she had enjoyed her afternoon. She told him that she had, advised him that his first patient was in the waiting room and retired to her own small room. Benedict only put in a brief appearance. The day, in consequence, seemed dull and uninteresting, stretching before her unendingly. But it finished at last. She was tidying up after the early evening surgery when the telephone rang and she went to answer it with some hesitation, for she felt herself quite inadequate for all but the simplest of calls. She lifted the receiver and uttered a cautious 'Hullo.'

Benedict's voice, brisk and friendly, answered her. 'Cassandra? Are you almost ready to leave? I thought we might have an evening together. Wear the new dress. I'll be at Mevrouw Schat's at seven o'clock.'

He rang off before she could reply; she put down the receiver assuring herself that if she had been given the opportunity to speak she would at least have made a show of refusing; wasn't he taking her for granted? Upon reflection she had to admit that he wasn't; her face warmed at the recollection of her warm response to his kisses—he must feel very sure of her. She sighed; at least she could give the new dress a second airing. She whisked around, putting things to rights at top speed, and within minutes was crunching through the snow to Mevrouw Schat's cheerfully lighted front door.

She was ready by the time he arrived, the new dress covered with her tweed coat and gloved and booted against the cold. Beyond a friendly 'Hullo, my girl,' he had nothing to say. Not until they were in the Aston Martin, driving out of Rhenen and turning off to go up the hill did he remark laconically, 'Dinner at De Koerheuval unless you'd prefer somewhere else?' and he didn't speak again as the car skidded up the narrow lane.

'Stay where you are,' he told her as he brought the car to a halt, got out and came round the car to open her door. 'Here, let me take your arm.' They made their way across the icy expanse towards the hotel entrance, their breath clouding the air around them, sliding and slipping and laughing until all at once Benedict stopped and pulled her close and kissed her with a warmth which set her heart pounding. Cassandra stood within the circle of his arm, oblivious of the wind and a few reluctant snowflakes, her candid eyes searching his face. 'In the office this morning,' she said thoughtfully, 'you were—I could have been a stranger, someone you were just being polite to. And now…'

'Now I'm kissing you as though I'm enjoying it, which I am. It would hardly do, my dear girl, if I were to kiss you each time we met in the surgery.'

Cassandra frowned. 'Oh,' she said coolly, 'you're thinking of what the patients might think.'

He laughed and tucked her arm more firmly into his. 'Don't be an idiot, I'm not thinking anything of the sort, and you know that well enough.' He kissed her again, quite roughly, and walked her briskly into the hotel.

They dined without haste in the restaurant, off game soup, roast beef and crêpes Suzette. There weren't a great many people there and they wouldn't have noticed anyway. A little light-headed from the wine, Cassandra, glowing with the knowledge that the dress really did do something for her, listened to Benedict's gentle flow of talk, which, while he never actually put it into words, seemed to include her in a future which was becoming rosier at every minute. It was after eleven when they finally got up to go. They hardly spoke as Benedict gentled the car down the hill. It was a clear night with stars twinkling in the frosty air, a cold moon sailing among them. Cassandra, staring around her, speaking her thoughts aloud, said: 'I wonder if it's like this on Mull. Ogre's Relish would be lovely...'

'You liked it there, didn't you, Cassandra?'

'Very much.' She glanced at him. 'And you—you didn't, of course...'

'Not at first, it was lonely, and then you came. Do you want to go back one day?'

'But I am going back.' Surely he must have known that? 'I must go somewhere while I find a job.' She made her voice sound reasonable and as casual as possible, hoping that he would contradict her. He didn't, said merely, 'Oh, yes, of course—but surely you'll wait until after Christmas?'

Cassandra swallowed her disappointment. 'Oh, yes, of course, I expect I'll stay for two or three weeks.'

He didn't seem to want to know more than that, for he said, 'You're free tomorrow afternoon, aren't you? Van Tromp tells me he's going to den Haag and hasn't any patients. Would you like to come to Utrecht? I'm going to operate.'

She said in a surprised voice, 'But you can't! It's too soon, Dr Viske said...'

'One case, that's all—an excision of larynx—a CA, of course. It's not been possible to use radium and if we do it now, we might get at it in time— even save the larynx.'

'But you might harm your eyes...'

'Not very likely, and it's a risk I choose to take. The patient is an old friend of mine.'

She could see that it was useless to try and dissuade him. 'I shall enjoy seeing you at work and I'd like to come very much. How happy you must feel to be back in your own world again—it must have seemed like a bad dream—at Ogre's Relish, I mean.'

'A dream, but not a bad one. I met you, remember?'

She answered him almost reluctantly. 'Yes. It's funny to think that we might never have met. Have you a great many friends, Benedict?'

He had been going slowly; now he pulled into the side of the deserted road and turned to look at her. 'A great many,' he assured her, and she couldn't see the little smile curving his mouth. 'But none of the women of my acquaintance—and you are interested in the women, aren't you?—would have borne with me on Mull. They wouldn't have stood my bad temper, nor would they have allowed me to indulge my ill-humour upon them, and certainly not one of them would have made me a cake.'

'No? But that doesn't matter now—you're not ill-humoured any more because you don't have any reason to be. I think,' she went on gravely, 'that they would be much more fun to take out than me.'

'It depends on your idea of fun, doesn't it?'

She was nothing if not persistent. 'But there must be someone special.'

His voice was bland. 'But of course there is, dear girl—I am, how shall I say, hindered by circumstances.'

Of course he meant Paula. What could be more hindering than to have your best friend marry the girl you wanted to marry yourself? She asked in a little voice, 'Couldn't you do anything about it?'

'No—and now I'm going to take you home.' He

started the car and she sat silent and snubbed. He'd asked her out for the evening because she was a willing buffer between him and loneliness, between him and the thought of Paula. She supposed, miserably, that he kissed her for the same reason.

They were almost at his house when she said, 'I'd like to go straight to Mevrouw Schat's if you don't mind.'

'I do mind.' He stopped the car outside his own door and was already getting out. 'You're coming in for coffee.'

'No, thank you—I'm going straight home to bed.'

'A remark which tempts me to an unsuitable reply. However, I'll not do that; I'll invite you in for coffee instead.'

She gave up. 'Well, all right, just for a few minutes.' She frowned. 'It's very late.'

'My reputation is a sound one, and so, I imagine, is yours. Hurry up, girl, it's cold!'

Jan must have been waiting in the hall, because he opened the door as they reached it and they had barely reached the sitting-room before Miep was there with a tray of coffee. Benedict, helping Cassandra out of her coat, bent to murmur in her ear,

'You see, Miss Prissy, how mindful I am of your out-of-date and endearing ideas about young ladies visiting men after midnight! Here we have a veritable battery of chaperons—you see, I took steps...'

Cassandra gave him a withering look. 'How detestable you are!' she said crossly, and went to sit by

Tante Beatrix, who wanted to know what they had eaten for dinner and where they had been and whether it was cold outside. 'It will be a cold Christmas,' she informed her listeners. 'Such a pity neither of you will be here. I shall be with cousin Karel in Doorn, of course, and you—you will be back for New Year, Benedict?'

He smiled at her. 'Unless my plans go awry—it is a little too soon for me to know.'

'And Cassandra?'

Before she could open her mouth, Benedict said carelessly, 'Oh, she will be on Mull, entertaining the reverend for tea and keeping an eye on Ogre's Relish.' He glanced across the room at her. 'Or won't you, Cassandra?'

'I have no idea,' she told him with faint bewilderment, 'what I shall be doing, only that I shall be there.' She finished her coffee and got up. 'I mustn't keep you out of bed any longer, Mevrouw van Manfeld,' she said, and found it disappointing when Benedict expressed no regret at her going but fetched her coat at once, shouted something to Jan as they passed through the hall, and stowed her away in the car in a businesslike manner. Outside Mevrouw Schat's front door she thanked him for a delightful evening and put her hand on the door, to have it imprisoned at once by his. 'Very delightful,' he agreed easily. 'We must do it again. Tomorrow evening—supposing we go to Utrecht and sample the bright lights?'

She felt an aching pity for him because he couldn't face being alone.

'Yes—no, well, I don't know.'

'A lucid answer!' His voice was lightly teasing. 'In that case come and have dinner with us at home, and I promise I'll be there.'

'Yes, but I'm going to watch you operate in the afternoon.'

He shook with laughter. 'Meaning that I shall put you off your dinner? That's harsh judgment, and no mistake; I always fancied myself rather a neat surgeon.'

She laughed with him and he remarked, 'That's better, you've not done that all day—you were very brisk this morning, did you know?' He got out to open her door. 'Will you be ready at half past one sharp? The list's at three o'clock, but I must allow for the state of the roads.'

He went to the door with her and opened it with the key Mevrouw Schat had given her, then gave her a little push. 'Inside with you, girl—goodnight.' He could have been a brother, a cousin, a very old friend from his manner, which further endorsed her guess that he had invited her because he couldn't bear to be alone.

She was waiting, nicely made up, her hair smooth under the fur cap, her boots beautifully polished, when Benedict arrived next day. The weather had brightened a little, but the roads were still treacherous, but once on the motorway, there was nothing to hinder them until they reached Utrecht where they were slowed almost to a walking pace by the mass of traffic.

At the hospital, Benedict led the way to the theatre block, large and modern and on the first floor. There were four theatre suites, he told an interested Cassandra, one of which was for ENT work, of which it seemed a great deal was done throughout the year, largely by himself. Cassandra, trying to see every-thing at once, went through the door into the block and led by Benedict, entered a small office. A pretty creature was sitting at the desk, curly-haired and blue-eyed and on excellent terms with Benedict, for she jumped up as he went in, laughing and talking and shaking his hand. Cassandra eyeing her covertly, wondered why it was that Benedict hadn't fallen for such a ravishing creature, but it was obvious, even to her jealous eye, that he hadn't. He greeted her with off-hand good humour and said in English, 'I've brought a visitor, so polish up your English, Bep,' and introduced the two girls. Having done so he put a careless hand on Cassandra's shoulder, 'Come back here afterwards and wait for me,' he told her, and went away.

The two girls were left together, but not for long, because Bep had to scrub to take the case and Cas-sandra had to be shown to the gallery, where, in the company of a number of students, she was to watch the operation. She had been advised by Bep to re-move her outdoor things and don a white gown, and now she sat, in the front row, looking down into the operating theatre.

The patient was already on the table and Bep, in her green gown and masked, was busy with her instruments. Benedict came presently, also gowned and masked, and the little group of people who had been waiting for him rearranged themselves into a pattern round the table with Benedict as their centre pin. He said something to the anaesthetist as a nurse started to arrange the towels and the sound of laughter floated upwards, and Cassandra, listening to it, smiled to herself. It seemed such a short time since Benedict had been walking with slow deliberation with his questing stick and his dark glasses, and now here he was, his sight quite restored, doing the work he loved. She wondered if he felt as happy about it as she did, and as though she had spoken aloud and he had heard her, he looked up to the gallery, sweeping it slowly with a searching gaze; he allowed it to rest on her when he found her and then turned away and picked up his scalpel. Suddenly she wanted to be down there with him, doing Bep's work, helping him, obeying his every wish, anticipating his needs, standing close to him—she suppressed a sigh and settled herself to watch.

He was good, she could see that. Unhurried and calm, almost casual in his movements. His voice, explaining each stage of the operation, sounded quiet and deliberate; it was a pity that she was unable to follow any of it, for he spoke in Dutch. He was dissecting the growth now, millimetre by careful millimetre. One slip of his scalpel and the operation would be a failure—not, she told herself robustly, that that would happen, there was no question of him failing. There wasn't— She watched one of the nurses step forward with a receiver and heard the gentle clang of the forceps as he dropped the result of his meticulous work into it. There was a little sigh around her as he did so, a sigh of applause and relief from the students watching. It was followed by a gentle shuffling of feet and easing of tense bodies as they settled to watch the remainder of the operation.

When it was at last over, she watched Benedict leave the theatre and then found her way back to Bep's office where she shed her gown, put on her coat and cap and started to do her face. She was using her lipstick when Benedict came in, still in his theatre gear although he had pulled off his cap and mask. He said 'Hullo' and smiled at her, and she, hardly knowing what she was doing, cast down the lipstick and flew into his arms. 'Oh, Benedict, I'm so happy—it was wonderful—I'm so proud!' She beamed up at him, her face alight with the feelings she had forgotten to hide.

And he for his part swung her off her feet, laughing out loud. 'What excitement, my dear girl, you're worse than a firecracker! I saw you, sitting up in the gallery in your white gown, and it's a good thing I did, for I promised myself I wouldn't start until I had.'

She was on her feet again, looking up at him. 'Why?'

'Because I knew you would bring me good luck, or give me strength, or whatever it is I need, and you did. You're my mascot.' He stood, with his hands in his pockets, his gown bunched up, laughing at her. 'We're going to have tea now and then we'll go back home, but first I must go and take a look at the patient. You'll wait?'

She would have waited for ever, but that wasn't something she would tell him, and the waiting didn't seem long anyway, because everyone else came in then, and there was plenty of talk which an English-speaking colleague of Benedict's translated for her. When Benedict returned, there was a great deal more talk until he asked if she was ready to go, when he swept her back through the long grey corridors to where the car was standing.

Because she really wanted to know, he explained the operation he had performed as they drove back to Rhenen; he had only just finished when they arrived outside the house and he said, laughing, 'What a waste of time when there are so many other things to talk about!' He smiled gently. 'Would you like to come in?'

Cassandra shook her head. 'No, I won't, thank you. There's an evening surgery and I like to get there in good time because I'm still a little slow.'

So he went on to Mevrouw Schat's little house and

dropped her off, saying as he started the engine
again, 'I'll walk around about seven.'

She said a little shyly, 'I'll be ready by then, but
I could quite easily…'

He ignored this. 'If the weather is really bad I'll
bring the car,' he told her as he drove away.

Cassandra saw a good deal of Benedict during the
next two days; he seemed to have an instinct for
knowing the exact moment in which she would finish
work, and if he took it for granted that she wished
to spend her evenings in his company she refused to
allow it to spoil them. She might only be second best,
but at least, just for a time she meant something to
him.

It was on the third day, just as she had poured
coffee for Mijnheer van Tromp, that he came in to
consult with his partner. She poured coffee for him
too and then went to answer the telephone. It was
for him; she handed him the receiver with a little
smile and sat down to drink her own coffee. She
wasn't listening, it was a meaningless jumble of
sound anyway, until he exclaimed in undisguised
delight, 'Paula!' She would have given a great deal
to have understood what he was saying then, for
something Paula had told him over the telephone had
made him a very happy man. It was quite some time
before he put the receiver down and made some remark to Mijnheer van Tromp.

'I thought that Paula was flying to Canada today,'
observed his partner.

Benedict stirred his coffee. 'The whole thing,' he said with quiet satisfaction, 'is off. She won't be going.'

Cassandra put down her cup and on the plea of work to do, got away. There was in fact, nothing to do, she sat behind the desk in the small room and allowed her thoughts to roam. It was all so clear. Benedict had never wanted Paula to go away and marry his best friend, but that very fact had made him stand aside when her choice had fallen on the other man. Now Paula, at the last minute, had changed her mind, hadn't he told them it was all off? So he would get his Paula after all—it didn't bear thinking of. It was a relief when the next patient arrived and gave her something to do.

She was to spend the evening with Benedict—dinner in Arnhem, he had said, despite the weather; now perhaps he wouldn't want to go, but a few minutes later, when he left, he reminded her carelessly to be ready for him when he called and went away before she could so much as nod. But before the end of the day, she managed to discover from her employer that Paula was at The Hague and would probably stay overnight. He offered her this information readily enough in answer to her roundabout questions, giving her a very old-fashioned look as he did so, but she was far too pre-occupied to notice; she was thinking that after this evening she might never go out with Benedict again. She promised herself that it should be a gay one and that she wouldn't remember

that sobering fact once. But when he came for her
and asked her if she would mind very much dining
at his home, in a faintly irritable manner, she saw
that he wasn't feeling gay at all, and made haste to
agree cheerfully.

In the hall, taking off her coat, she managed to
take a quick look at him; he seemed tired and
strained and decidedly bad-tempered and her heart
sank. Naturally he was annoyed because he couldn't
spend the evening with Paula, but surely he could
have driven over to The Hague? Perhaps she should
have pleaded a headache and left him his evening
free. In the sitting-room she asked bluntly, 'Have you
a headache—are your eyes bothering you?' She ignored his annoyed glance. 'Perhaps you should be
wearing your glasses—did you operate again today?'

He handed her a glass of sherry and said, far too
smoothly, 'I'm perfectly all right. You ask far too
many questions, Cassandra, but if you must know I
have had rather a heavy day.'

Over the dining-table, Cassandra was relieved to
see that Benedict's mood lightened. That he was still
preoccupied was still very evident, but at least he
made conversation with his two companions. It was
unfortunate that Cassandra, over one of Miep's delicious soufflés, felt emboldened to ask if he would
be operating on the following day.

She hadn't expected the ferocious expression upon
his face nor the curtness of his 'No.' She gaped at
him, so surprised that she would probably have said

something foolish if Mevrouw van Manfeld hadn't at that precise moment asked about an old friend of hers who had gone to Mijnheer van Tromp's consulting rooms that day. There seemed to be quite a lot to say about her, and it seemed a natural thing for the old lady to reminisce about various of her acquaintances, so she kept the conversation firmly in her hands for the rest of dinner, while they drank their coffee afterwards, and when she had at length finished, she fixed Cassandra with a sharp, elderly eye, and inquired of her if she was not tired.

It was an opening Cassandra had been hoping for, she said at once that yes, she was, and would anyone mind if she went home. Tante Beatrix nodded approval but Benedict frowned. 'It's early,' he declared, for all the world, thought Cassandra, as though the evening had been a roaring success instead of several painful hours of rather forced chat between herself and Tante Beatrix, while Benedict sat silent.

She summoned a smile to answer him. 'Yes, you must forgive me,' and got to her feet, and when he made no rise too, 'No, don't get up. Jan told me that he wanted to see Mevrouw Schat about something or other and he might as well walk back with me now.' It was distinctly disconcerting when he agreed to this without any hesitation whatever and no sign of regret.

She didn't see Benedict all next day, and when, during the evening surgery, she cautiously inquired

of his partner as to his whereabouts, it was to learn
that he had gone to Utrecht and would probably stay
the night. Mijnheer van Tromp had looked at her
keenly as he spoke, but she had pretended not to see
the look but had asked with elaborate carelessness:

'He seemed delighted to hear that Paula had can-
celled her trip to Canada.' There was no solace to be
got from his cheerful:

'Yes—an unexpected last-minute decision—they
have been close friends for years, you know. Paula
is a delightful young woman, she will make an excellent wife for a medical man.'

It was an unhappy thought to carry with her
through the long day, and the following day too. And
it had made it no easier when Paula arrived unex-
pectedly during the afternoon. She had looked upset,
almost tearful, and although she had smiled at Cassandra she had paused only long enough to say that
Mijnheer van Tromp was expecting her and could
she go straight in?

And on her way out, a long half hour later, she
had stopped again and said rapidly, 'Just as all the
plans were made, and now poor Benedict has to face
up to it all over again!'

Cassandra murmured suitably. She presumed that
Paula was referring to the wedding arrangements and
was on the point of making some remark to this effect when she was summoned by Mijnheer van
Tromp. She wished Paula a rather hurried good-bye
and went along to the consulting room.

If she had hoped to hear something about Paula and Benedict she was disappointed, for the summons was in order to ask her if she would escort a nervous patient to the hospital in Utrecht on the following afternoon. She was to have an intravenous pylogram and had agreed to having it done provided she had a nurse with her the whole time. Cassandra agreed readily enough; she saw no reason to think that an IVP would be done any differently from the usual procedure in England, so probably she would have nothing to do but keep close to the patient and soothe her when necessary.

They went at once to the X-ray department when they reached the hospital, and Cassandra found to her relief that it was the counterpart of her own hospital in London. She stayed with her patient while the dio- done was injected and then remained with her while the X-rays were taken, a business lasting half an hour or so, and while they were being developed, the lady becoming restless and bored, insisted upon Cassan- dra going to the hospital entrance to make sure that the car was ready and waiting. She got lost almost immediately and when she retraced her steps went to the left instead of the right; a passage with doors along one side and a blank wall on the other. She was halfway down it when a door she was passing was flung open and Benedict came out with Mijnheer Viske and the radiologist on his heels. He stopped short when he saw her and his eyes narrowed so that she looked quite guilty and took a couple of steps backwards. He said in a nasty voice, 'Well, if it isn't Miss Nosey Parker! What curious coincidence brings you here? Don't tell me that you have added listening at keyholes to your other talents?'

Cassandra was thunderstruck. 'Me?' Her voice rose and became rather loud. 'You must be out of your mind, or joking! I hadn't the least idea that you were here, and if I had I certainly shouldn't have come looking for you. And how,' she continued furiously, 'can I listen at keyholes if I can't understand a word of your language?' She glared at him, in a fine rage. 'I'm with a patient, if you must know, and I haven't the least interest in your activities, Mijnheer van Manfeld.'

Nicely primed with ill-temper, she sailed past him, only to find that the passage came to an end against a blank wall. She would have to turn round and go back, past them all.

'And where are you going?' asked Mijnheer van Manfeld in a very quiet voice.

'To the entrance.' She was already on her way back, but now he was standing in her path. 'I came down the wrong passage...'

It was Mijnheer Viske who stepped between them, saying kindly, 'Such an easy thing to do—I'll show you, Nurse,' and walked her back to the main corridor and pointed out the right corner to turn. Still quivering with the strength of her feelings, she found her way easily enough then, delivered her message, and went back to her patient. There was no sign of

Benedict this time, only, as she hurried along, she thought she heard his voice through one of the closed doors.

Her patient dozed on the return journey and she had plenty of time to think, so that by the time they had arrived back at her companion's house and she had seen her safely inside its door, she had quite made up her mind what she was going to do. She would go and see Benedict; just because he was to have his Paula after all was no reason for being so ill-tempered. She suspected that he might be feeling guilty about herself—after all, he had taken her out a good many times—and kissed her; she went vividly pink remembering how willingly she had kissed him in return—she would have to make him understand that she hadn't taken any of it seriously, that it had been nothing more than a pleasant friendship, she might even invent a mythical boy-friend—John Campbell, for instance; then perhaps they could return to their old friendly footing and at least part on good terms.

It seemed good sense to strike while the iron was hot; she walked round to Benedict's house, rang the old-fashioned brass bell and was admitted by Jan. She stayed a few minutes to talk to him and then asked:

'I came to see Mijnheer van Manfeld, Jan. Is he here?'

He nodded, his black eyes without expression. 'In the library, Miss Cassandra,' and she had the impression that he wished to say more, but wouldn't. When he remained silent she went on, 'Do you suppose I could have a word with him?'

For answer he led the way across the hall and knocked on the door, opened it, murmured something and ushered her in. Benedict was standing with his back to the fire, his face in shadow, for the only light in the room was from a small table lamp in one corner and the flickering fire itself. He said with casual politeness, 'Hullo, Cassandra—this is an unexpected pleasure,' his cool tones belying his words so that she had a strong urge to turn tail again. But that would be silly now that she had got so far. She came a little further into the room and began without preamble:

'It's a little difficult, but there's something I want to say—I daresay once I get started it will be all right.' She paused and eyed him doubtfully and he said, still very polite, 'Why not sit down? We might as well talk in comfort,' but she shook her head. He shrugged indifferent shoulders. 'Of course, I owe you an apology for this afternoon—I had no right to speak as I did,' his voice was stiff, like a stranger's. 'I was extremely—er—put out about something, and seeing you just at that very moment…poor Cassandra.'

She would have preferred him to have shouted at her, to have called her Miss Busybody, even to have sworn at her; it would have seemed more like him.

This courteous man, calling her poor Cassandra, didn't seem like Benedict at all. She tried again.

'I can quite understand why you are avoiding me, but it's quite unnecessary, you know. We've been friends, after a fashion, but knowing each other hasn't anything to do with your life here—your personal life, I mean.' She stopped, because it sounded muddled even in her own ears, but it would have to do. He must surely understand. 'We only met by chance,' she reminded him, and looked at him hopefully, because he could help her out if he wished. But all he said, a smile tugging at the corner of his mouth, was, 'Chance? Cassandra by chance?'

She took no notice of this trivial remark, for she was keyed up to say her piece and she was going to say it, come what may. 'I quite understand that you needed someone to—to talk to when you were so unhappy, but now you and Paula—I'm so glad,' she added breathlessly. 'So you see you have no reason to hide away from me and be so angry when you meet me, and I'm going back to England soon anyway…I'd much rather leave as friends.'

He had turned away, so that all she could see of his face was his profile. 'You really believe that—about Paula and myself?' he sounded thoughtful. 'Well, I suppose you might as well believe that as anything.'

Cassandra hardly heard him; she was too occupied in keeping her matter-of-fact manner. 'Well, that's all right then; I've enjoyed being here—it was quite

an experience.' And I can say that again, she told
herself silently, and moved back towards the door.
'I've things to do,' she informed him brightly. 'I really must go.' Her hand sought and found the door
knob behind her, and with a vacuous "Bye for now,'
she made her awkward exit.

Jan was in the hall. She wished him goodnight, the
bright smile she had pinned to her white face making
it a sorry sight. He shut the steel door behind her and
went straight back to the library. He knocked and
went in and addressed his master's back.

'Miss Cassandra is upset, Mijnheer,' he stated with
the directness of an old friend. 'Her poor face—it is
stiff with unhappiness.'

Benedict turned round to face him. He said savagely, 'And what am I supposed to do about that,
my good Jan? After all this time of patient waiting—
and I had to be sure, you will grant me that. Do you
really suppose I would ask her to share the life of a
blind man? You know what Viske told me this afternoon. No, far better that she goes back to Mull
without knowing—she's got hold of some cock-and-
bull story about Paula and myself—let her believe
it.' He took his dark glasses out of his pocket and
put them on impatiently. 'And not a word to her,
Jan—I have your promise.'

'You have, Mijnheer, and I understand how you
feel. I also understand that Miss Cassandra's heart
will break...'

Benedict said something explosive. 'Get out, my old friend,' he advised, 'before I do you an injury.'

Cassandra walked briskly back to Mevrouw Schat's house, temporarily uplifted by her action, but by the time she was seated in the little parlour, the uplift had gone, leaving her feeling cold and sick inside so that her landlady's *hutspot*, just right for a cold winter's evening, congealed on her plate. She pleaded a headache presently and went to her room and had a good cry, which while not improving the situation one jot, at least relieved her feelings.

She was, to all appearances, her own self in the morning, and if she didn't laugh quite as readily as usual at Mijnheer van Tromp's little jokes, he didn't appear to notice, and when at the end of the morning he called her into his consulting room and told her that the new nurse would be coming in two days' time, Cassandra was able to receive the news with equanimity, agreeing to his suggestion that she should leave on the evening of her successor's arrival, telling herself that it was a very good thing considering the awkwardness of her relationship with Benedict.

Mijnheer van Tromp intended to take her to Schipol himself; she would go to London and spend a couple of days there, shopping and getting used to a world which no longer held Benedict. Time enough to telephone Rachel when she was in England. She would go and say good-bye to him, but not until the last minute, and there was plenty to keep her busy for the next day. It was fortunate that the afternoon was booked solid and she had no time to think about herself at all, and the next day she had to pack and get everything in apple-pie order for the new nurse.

It was evening when she went round to Benedict's house for the last time. Jan opened the door and ushered her inside with his usual fatherly manner and offered to take her coat.

She looked round a little nervously. It was far worse than a visit to the dentist; she wondered if she had been wise to come after all. Supposing she were to burst into tears or say something for which she would be sorry later? She said hastily: 'No, thank you, Jan. I only came to say good-bye.'

He inclined his head sadly. 'We had heard, Miss Cassandra, and very sorry we are to hear it.'

'I'm sorry to go, Jan, it's nice of you to mind too...I just wanted to say good-bye to Mijnheer van Manfeld. He's home?'

His black eyes were blank. 'No, miss, he's been away for the last two days, and I can't say when he will be back.'

'Away?' She hadn't thought of that, now she wouldn't see him again. She swallowed the tears crowding her throat. 'I'm sorry. May I see Mevrouw van Manfeld?'

The old lady was in the sitting-room, the cat on her knee. 'He misses Benedict,' she explained, 'and so do I, but I daresay he will be back shortly. Very urgent business, he told me, my dear, and I didn't ask him about it, for he was in one of his black moods.'

Cassandra had stooped to tickle the cat's chin; she straightened suddenly. 'His glasses,' she said urgently, 'was he wearing his glasses again?'

The old lady looked a little startled. 'Why, no, my dear, because I asked him if he had forgotten them and he said something quite regrettable about spectacles and his dark ones in particular. He begged my pardon at once.' She peered at Cassandra, who was prowling round the room, quite unable to sit down. 'Why do you ask, Cassandra?'

'It was only an idea—that his eyes might be bad again, but if he wasn't wearing his dark glasses it couldn't be that.' She came to a halt before Mevrouw van Manfeld. 'I came to say good-bye.'

Tante Beatrix said gently, 'Yes, dear, I knew about it. I shall miss you and I'm sorry to see you go. You have been good for Benedict; not silly and selfish like all those other girls who used to come and see him. He would take them out to dinner and they would bore him stiff—so he told me—pleasant enough company, but only after him for his money. You aren't afraid of him either, nor do you care when he loses his temper.'

Cassandra could think of nothing suitable to say in reply. She smiled and nodded and kissed the old lady's cheek, then went to find Miep and Jan. As he was seeing her to the door she said, 'You will take care of him, Jan? And when he comes back will you

wish him good-bye from me, and all the happiness
in the world?'

Jan stared at her, on the point of saying something,
but when he nodded silently she turned away, to stop
as he asked, 'You'll be writing when you get back
to Mull, Miss Cassandra?'

'I don't think so, Jan—perhaps, later.' She went
back to him and kissed his leathery cheek. 'Bless
you, Jan. I'm going to miss you.'

'And Mijnheer?'

'All the rest of my life, Jan.'

CHAPTER NINE

THE drive back to Schipol took rather longer than Cassandra had expected, for the snow, although it had been cleared from the main roads, hampered the car's progress on the by-ways which Mijnheer van Tromp had decided to take so that she might see a little more of Holland. That the flat white expanse around them offered no view of anything at all, seemed to have escaped him, and for her it couldn't have mattered less, for while she maintained a comfortably desultory conversation with her companion she endeavoured to get her thoughts into some kind of order.

She was fairly satisfied that she had left her job in a fit state for the new nurse, a pleasant girl who, she felt sure, was going to do the work far better than she herself had done. She had said good-bye to everyone; Mevrouw Schat, the secretary who worked for Mijnheer van Tromp, everyone, in fact, save Benedict, who had apparently disappeared and left no clue as to his whereabouts. And yet when she had asked her employer if he had mentioned her departure to his partner she had been told that yes, certainly he had informed him, but something in Mijnheer van Tromp's face had warned her not to ask any more questions. She sat pondering Benedict's behaviour, consoling herself that at least he had never discovered that she loved him, and even if he did, it didn't matter any more.

The airport was busy; its lights blazed in the early evening dark, a constant stream of people going to and fro, clutching children, parcels intended for Christmas, and extra coats and wraps, gave the whole place an air of excited expectancy. She wished Mijnheer van Tromp good-bye, uttered a few empty phrases about seeing him again, put her case on the conveyor belt and walked towards the reception desk; the quicker she got over the leaving part the better. It was at the passport check that the pleasant young man behind the desk asked her with smiling politeness if she would be so good as to step on one side. She did so, wondering why and voicing uncertainty as to her luggage. The young man made a soothing reply, nodded to a fellow Customs officer to take his place, and ushered her through a door behind the desk. It opened on to a long dreary passage which apparently led nowhere and Cassandra came to a halt.

'I should like to know what I've done or what has happened before I go any further,' she stated positively, 'and you've got my passport.'

He handed it back to her with a word of apology. 'There is nothing wrong,' he told her in slow English. 'If you would just come with me—not far.' He smiled encouragingly and Cassandra started walking again, a little reluctantly. After a minute she said, 'But what about my luggage? And my flight goes in less than ten minutes.'

'Rest assured that everything is OK, miss.' His voice was friendly. 'Through this door, if you would be so good...'

He opened the heavy wooden door as he spoke and she found herself outside in a narrow road leading, she supposed, to some sort of car park. She looked inquiringly at her companion and then turned in time to see the Aston Martin creep to a halt before her. She was staring at it open-mouthed when Benedict got out, said something to the young man and walked towards her, and when the young man wished her good-bye and offered a hand to be shaken, she did so mechanically and she didn't see him go. Only the door shutting with a click recalled her to where she was. 'There's been some mistake,' she mumbled. 'My luggage—the plane...'

Benedict was standing close to her. 'Of course there has been a mistake,' he agreed genially. 'There have been several mistakes—all mine—but this, my dearest darling, is no mistake.'

Cassandra was in his arms and being kissed. It went on for some time and when he at last loosened his hold, just a little, she said desperately:

'You must explain—I don't understand...'

'My darling. I'll explain as we go, and all you have to understand is that I love you.' He opened the door of the car and she found herself getting in. 'My luggage?' she asked weakly.

'We'll buy a toothbrush,' he promised her, and got in beside her and started to drive away.

They were on the E10, the motorway taking them to Rotterdam, before she said in a little voice, 'Benedict, I must know—I don't even know where we're going.'

'The Hoek, my love—to catch the night ferry. We can just about get to Mull by tomorrow evening.'

'Mull?' she echoed stupidly.

'Christmas with your sister. Do you suppose she will invite me if I ask her?'

There was a short silence while Cassandra, her wits addled, digested this. 'Paula?' she asked at length.

'My dear darling, Paula will be married before the New Year.'

'Yes, but you let me think that you and she—when I came to see you and you were b-beastly...'

He took a hand briefly from the steering wheel and laid it over hers.

'Cassandra, you remember when we met in the hospital, and I was cruel—Viske had just told me that it seemed possible that I was going to lose my sight again. You were quite right when you asked me if my eyes were troubling me. There were, only I wouldn't admit it. You see, I had waited all those weeks to be sure—how could I ask you to marry a man who could become blind? And then everything came right, didn't it? And just to be quite sure, I made myself wait just a little while longer, and on the very day I had promised myself that I would ask you to marry me, Viske telephoned to say that he had grave doubts, and so I let you go, believing that ridiculous story about Paula and me, and I must say, my darling, that a worse case of putting two and two together and making five I have yet to meet—and then, after two days in Utrecht with Viske, he finally decided this afternoon that there will be no permanent blindness, a chance of temporary weakness perhaps, from time to time, unless I'm careful…'

'Oh, darling Benedict, I'll see that you're careful,' said Cassandra huskily.

'Are you crying, darling Miss Darling?'

'Yes—no, not really. I mean, I'm so happy. Did Jan know?'

'Of course, and van Tromp. I telephoned him a few minutes before you left—and Jan, who promised to see about the boat for me.'

'But how did the Customs man know—he stopped me from going on board the plane.'

Benedict sounded pleased with himself. 'It just so happened that I did a rather tricky operation on him last year—remembered him just in time when I was wondering how to stop you.

'There are a lot of things I don't quite…'

He said decisively, 'We have all night on board to talk, my darling.'

He pulled the car off the road into a deserted lay-by and Cassandra asked, 'Why have we stopped?'

'Because before we go any further, my dearest, I think I should ask you to marry me. I must warn you that I shall probably be a very difficult man to live with, but at least I shall love you until the day I die, and beyond.'

'In that case,' said Cassandra without any hesitation whatever, 'I'll say yes.'

It was a few minutes later when she lifted her head from his shoulder to ask, 'But why were you so pleased when Paula told you she wasn't going to Canada?'

'Why, Jan had cabled her to say that he had the chance of a job in Utrecht and there was no need for her to go out there—they merely put off getting married until he returns in a few days' time.'

'Oh,' said Cassandra, 'I thought…'

'And now let us tear our thoughts away from Paula and Jan, my darling, and talk about us. There is a great deal to decide. We must get married…'

And they were, on a cold blustery January day in the little village church on Mull, with only a handful of family to see them wed, but the entire village filling its pews to capacity. The austere little building was overflowing with flowers and, Cassandra, walking down the aisle on Tom's arm, sniffed their scent appreciatively and caught Benedict's eye and smiled her thanks, for he had promised her that she should have all the flowers he could buy for their wedding and he had more than fulfilled his promise. He had given her a mink coat too. She was wearing it over the blue velvet dress she had gone to Edinburgh to buy—it had had to be blue because the ring he had given her was a sapphire. She had no doubt that he would give her anything she asked for and a lot more besides, and that was nice to know, but there was only one thing she wanted, and that was his love. She raised her nice hazel eyes to his grey ones and saw the love there, shining out at her.

The reception was at Rachel's house, a cheerful happy gathering where everyone knew everyone else and had a great deal to say in consequence. Which was probably why no one noticed when the bride and groom disappeared, to reappear very shortly, clad in sheepskin jackets and tweeds, looking for all the world as though they were going for an energetic hike, as indeed they were, for five minutes later, their brief good-byes said, they started up the path to Ogre's Relish. They paused to take their breath half way up and Cassandra said, 'We're a little mad, you know. People go to the south of France or Bournemouth or Paris for a honeymoon, and we choose to spend it in a cottage miles from anywhere—we'll have to wash up and cook and light the fires.'

Benedict laughed and hugged her close. 'I light a lovely fire,' he told her, 'and as for the rest, Jan has busied himself for days making things easy for us.'

They went on together, holding hands. 'Shall we

come here every year?' Cassandra wanted to know, as they were on the last leg of the path.

'Yes, why not? The children will have to pitch tents or swing hammocks.'

'How ever many?' she gasped.

'I hated being an only child, my darling, and I've money enough for a dozen.'

They stopped because Ogre's Relish was in sight. Someone had put the lights on, the windows shone a welcome, a wisp of smoke curled up from the chimney to get lost in the darkening sky.

'I'll tell you what,' said Cassandra, 'I'm prepared to compromise. How about half a dozen, assorted?'

They stood together at the end of the path, laughing, until Benedict caught her close and kissed her soundly before they walked, arm-in-arm, to the cottage door.

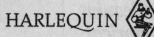

HARLEQUIN PRESENTS®

HARLEQUIN PRESENTS
men you won't be able to resist
falling in love with...

HARLEQUIN PRESENTS
women who have feelings
just like your own...

HARLEQUIN PRESENTS
powerful passion in
exotic international settings...

HARLEQUIN PRESENTS
intense, dramatic stories that will keep you
turning to the very last page...

HARLEQUIN PRESENTS
The world's bestselling romance series!

Harlequin® Historical

From rugged lawmen and
valiant knights to defiant heiresses
and spirited frontierswomen,
Harlequin Historicals will
capture your imagination with
their dramatic scope, passion
and adventure.

Harlequin Historicals...
they're too good to miss!

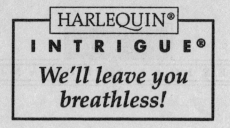

HARLEQUIN®
AMERICAN ◆ ROMANCE®

LOOK FOR OUR FOUR FABULOUS MEN!

Each month some of today's bestselling authors bring
four new fabulous men to Harlequin American Romance.
Whether they're rebel ranchers, millionaire power brokers
or sexy single dads, they're all gallant princes—and
they're all ready to sweep you into lighthearted fantasies
and contemporary fairy tales where anything is possible
and where all your dreams come true!

You don't even have to make a wish...
Harlequin American Romance will grant your every desire!

Look for Harlequin American Romance
wherever Harlequin books are sold!